# NETHER WORLD'S GATE

# Also by W.J. Cherf

## The Manuscripts of The Richards' Trust

## The Adventures of J.J. Stone

## Adventures in Paranormal Archaeology

# NETHER WORLD'S GATE

## ADVENTURES IN PARANORMAL ARCHAEOLOGY II

### BY

### W.J. CHERF

FBP

FOXBAT PUBLISHING

Copyright © 2018 William Joseph Cherf

Foxbat Publishing
ISBN: 978-0-9989318-9-0

Cover art and frontispiece. Image of KUR, the Sumerian snake-headed dragon. Cylinder seal and clay impression. Uruk style. *Ca.* 3000 BCE. Image courtesy of Marie-Lan Nguyen and PHGCOM via WikiMedia Commors. The artifact resides in the Louvre Museum, Paris.

# DEDICATION

Even though this is my tenth effort, I, as an author, remain deeply indebted to those who offer their invaluable criticism—both good and bad. The process of storytelling is an arduous and oftentimes treacherous one. It tests one's creativity, while stretching the mind. Frankly, I enjoy the process as it best reminds me of an ancient Japanese sword maker, who, layer upon layer, laboriously builds a resilient and flexible blade.

To the many members of the Fiction Foundry of Colorado Springs, Colorado, I extend my deepest thanks for your time and many fine insights and suggestions. To my beta-readers, Chris, and several others too shy to be named, words cannot express my gratitude. To my copy editor, Stephanie, thank you for your care and suggestions.

To Sweet Sue: I am very pleased that you liked this one. And as I have said many times before, your opinion is all that really matters.

# PROLOGUE

Within the temple's innermost sanctuary, an elderly Sumerian priest hovered over a silver basin. Its crystalline water slowly clouded to reveal a portent. As his heavily kohl-darkened eyes gazed into its depths, his arthritic hands trembled, his spotted, bald head creased with wide-eyed concern, and finally outright horror. Dark tendrils of evil reached out from the earth, spreading unchecked throughout the land. With a pallor the color of goat's milk, the priest gestured to his assistant. Tersely he said, "Immediately, call a priestly council. We have grave matters to discuss."

The following day, all thirty-seven members of the priesthood answered the old one's dire command. As their number formed, a low rumble of conversation resonated within the blue-glazed walls of the temple's outer sanctuary. In the sputtering lamplight, the raised-relief tiles depicting fearsome dragon-lions seemed to breathe fire and flick their tails with impatience. They too appeared to understand the gravity of the moment.

"Thank you, my brothers, for answering my call. I

have received a portent of great consequence. We have a crisis to forestall. In seven years' time, the earth will be torn asunder and the dark hordes of the Netherworld will be released upon our land. We must prevent this."

"How?" asked a colleague some twenty years his junior.

"We must journey forth with an astronomer, a scribe, architect, and foremen. Along the way, we must find the labor to construct an impervious barrier to seal over this coming rent in the earth."

"Where will this 'rent' appear?" asked another.

"Far to the west, beyond a great river, in a rocky desert. We will follow the caravan routes north and then west, and from there, the stars will guide us. They will show us the way. Without question, this journey will be long and arduous."

"Where will we find the required building material?" queried a third, an architect by trade.

"Our city's guardian, the blessed Goddess Nammu, creator of the world, will guide us as she always has," the old man stated with absolute conviction and a tight fist. "I suspect that we will find many eager allies among the Egyptians, who will help us complete this mission."

"Egyptians!" another retorted with a rude snort.

"Those bigoted and haughty non-believers! I will not help their kind or kin in any way." At the end of that tirade, the priest stormed off and left the others to stand and stare at each other.

Sensing the fast arrival of a crisis point, the old priest remarked, "It is true that our neighbors to the far west are arrogant. But we must see beyond this. The rent in the earth will take place in their land. Some among you might be tempted to say, 'let that be their burden'. But once the dark demons of the Netherworld are unleashed upon mortal kind, it would only be a brief matter of time before we *too* would be engulfed by their wretched hordes."

Now looking around, pausing to confront the face of each who remained, the old priest continued.

"I seek men to join me on this journey west. I seek not children who I must attend to," he said with a nod in the direction of the departed one.

After much discussion, it was agreed that an expedition of twenty would undertake the journey. The old seer, Giskhim by name, would lead it.

\* \* \*

Overland trade in the ancient Near East coursed along routes long-established since prehistoric times.

Giskhim's band began its journey by joining a caravan of donkeys and carts, which traveled north from the city state of Ur, along the western bank of the Euphrates River. After several days, they turned west and continued on across a vast wasteland to the Levantine coastline. While the route was indeed "long and arduous," dotted with solitary wells of odd-tasting water, they crossed without incident.

Upon reaching the Mediterranean, all gasped in wonder and awe for none could imagine such a vast, blue, watery expanse. Its cool and refreshing breezes buoyed their spirits greatly. Their journey south along the coastline took the Sumerian band past well-provisioned towns with great stone fortifications instead of mud brick, past harbor wharfs bustling with trade and filled with sailing ships from distant lands. This they noted by counting no less than six different styles of mast riggings. At every turn, a new marvel seemed to appear before them, so many they began to lose count.

Reaching the eastern frontier of the Egyptian delta, Giskhim's entourage passed from waterless desert to verdant cultivation as far as the eye could see. Many remarked upon this vision. Turning to their astronomer, a man named Tirigan, the old priest asked, "What is your reckoning of how far we have journeyed?"

Checking his tally on a clay ledger, the astronomer replied, "Seventy days have passed since we left our beloved Ur, Venerable One. A donkey's pace can be variable. So, to answer your question, Venerable One, a great distance," was the man's final answer, to which the old priest merely grunted.

A handful of days later, Giskhim and his fellow travelers reached Memphis, the capital, after passing by countless farm plots and lush groves of date palm trees ripe for picking. Here the expedition took in the city's great white fortification walls and its seemingly endless wharfs along a great but contrary river, which to the Sumerians, flowed in the wrong direction.

"How can this be?" One asked. "The rivers of our homeland flow opposite. I am confused."

Giskhim just smiled broadly. "Horgal, have you not already seen during our journey many wondrous things? This is yet another, my brother. Let us learn together as we did in scribal school."

That evening while sighting off the stars, their astronomer told the old priest that his goal was near—only one or two days away. For old Giskhim, already long weary of their trek, it had all seemed but a dream.

Their journey south now progressed by boat along the wide, but contrary river, and took them past many breathtaking marvels. Flocks of colorful water birds took to the skies at their approach, shading them with their passage. Flowers that floated on the water and covered the river's banks perfumed their noses. Beyond the bushy banks, they saw irrigated fields ripe with wheat and barley.

"This land seems all too perfect," another remarked. "Where are the armies stationed? These villages that we pass are without defenses. The entire land is one vast unmolested farmer's field."

"Do I detect jealously in your words, Senada?" the old priest observed.

In response, his colleague just shook his head.

But within the rushes that lined the river's banks lurked dangerous creatures, dark and treacherous-looking, with long mouths filled with teeth. These they liked to display proudly in the sun while tiny birds picked at morsels. Far more fearsome, the Sumerians noted that their boatman gave wide birth to a basking group of large and wallowing creatures, which floated with only the tops of their heads exposed. Occasionally, they would rise up, yawn their jaws wide, brandish their long curved teeth, and bellow. Never had the Sumerians seen or heard the like before.

Their river journey ended at a vast limestone

plateau that overlooked the river's course. Its western landings were busy with activity. Here the boatman proudly told the foreigners of the construction of the Pharaoh Djoser's mortuary buildings, which had begun under the watchful gaze of the king's master architect, Imhotep. This narration the scribe, Surgal, translated for the rest as best he could.

Leaving the river boat, Giskhim and his followers espied a vast artificial plain had been cleared atop the limestone plateau, upon which shallow water channels crisscrossed. As jugs of water filled the interconnected system, measurements were taken, and so by such a clever device did the workmen level the funerary structure's foundations.

The Sumerians, mesmerized by the scale of the undertaking, stood dumbly about in wonder.

"They all work as if of one mind," one remarked.

"None work under the lash," said another.

Interrupting this gawking gaggle of foreigners, the master architect Imhotep briskly strode over to confront them. In spite of his lofty station, the man wore a sweat-stained cloth head covering, a once white kilt marred with streaks of red surveying ochre, and common papyrus sandals.

"Who are you and from where do you come?" he

demanded with his hands on hips.

Giskhim, impressed by the man's demeanor, motioned to Surgal, who moved to Giskhim's side to act as his interpreter.

The old seer's words now reached the Egyptian's ears.

"Most honorable overseer, I am Giskhim of Ur." The priest bowed and gestured broadly, "We have traveled far and long to your land on an earnest mission. We have just paused here to marvel at your architectural skill."

The meaning of these words Imhotep had to piece together as Surgal's skills as an interpreter were not as good as the scribe thought. Taking in the old priest, Imhotep responded, "Most venerable Giskhim of Ur, I have heard of this faraway place. I can only imagine your journey." Now glancing up into the cloudless sky, "May I offer you and your company some refreshment and shade?"

"We would be so honored."

Imhotep's bandy legs quickly led the Sumerians to a viewing stage over which an awning was stretched. After the architect barked out several commands, numerous pillows appeared, as did many jugs of fresh, cool beer.

One of Giskhim's retinue whispered to another, "So much for the rumors of Egyptian rudeness and inhospitality."

Once everyone had been seated and refreshed, Giskhim addressed Imhotep. "Honorable One, your hospitality is most appreciated."

"Venerable One, you are most welcome, but my curiosity has been piqued. You mentioned you and your friends are on 'an earnest mission'. What is it?"

Giskhim looked down to his arthritic hands clutched in an attitude of prayer while he constructed his answer. *Most generous and wise Nammu, please guide my words.*

"Honorable Imhotep, several months ago I received a portent, which foretold an awful event. A tear will violently be made in the earth, which will open the Netherworld and allow the release of demons of pure evil. We, my fellow priests and I, wish to find this nearby place. Then when we locate it, we wish to build upon that spot an everlasting structure that will forever block evil from invading our world."

Imhotep sat impassively as he listened to the old priest's words. This seer, who had traveled so far and endured so much, all to address a dire prophecy. This awful thing the priest described, Imhotep knew Egypt's own high priests had predicted and worried over. But they lacked the horrific specifics that this Sumerian shared.

So, as was his way, the master architect asked bluntly, "Where is this place?"

Giskhim summoned to their circle of conversation the company's astronomer, Tirigan, who had been respectfully listening several feet away.

"My colleague, the Honorable Imhotep wishes to know the place which we seek."

Pointing in a westerly direction, the star-gazer said, "Over that rise, perhaps a day's walk from this place."

When told of this, Imhotep grunted, rubbed at the stubble on his chin, and said, "I know of this place. Tomorrow I will take you there. Tonight, you and your fellow priests will be my honored guests."

*   *   *

The following day, true to his word, Imhotep led the Sumerians up and around several rises in the terrain to the west of the building activity. Again traveling by donkey, the ride inland led to a sandy depression surrounded by rocky hills. The old seer sensed in his bones the rightness of the place upon seeing it and promptly felt a mild trembling beneath him. Falling off his donkey, Giskhim felt dizzy at the confusion to his inner ear.

Seeing the Sumerian's reaction, Imhotep laughed. "Venerable Giskhim! What you just felt was the earth god Geb's own laughter. This entire region suffers from it! As a result, my draftsmen and workmen struggle mightily each day to keep their figures accurate and survey lines straight."

After the trembling stopped, the Sumerian quickly gathered himself, stood, and trod toward the sandy depression before him. Stopping, the seer then declared to all, "The rent will be here, beneath my feet."

Extending his arms out, "Our structure must course along this line for at least forty paces, with a proportional width pleasing to the gods. It must be built of an everlasting stone—not of mud brick."

Imhotep, impressed by the old priest's certitude, asked, "When will this calamity occur?"

Calculating against Tirigan's notations, the seer said, "Six years, seven months, and fourteen days from now."

Imhotep grunted from atop his donkey, turned this way and that, and said, "Venerable One, you will need a rubble causeway to move building material upon. Next, you must send masons far upriver to find the 'everlasting' material you require. Once quarried, that material must be sent upriver by boat, hauled to this site, placed, and dressed. But beforehand, you must prepare a foundation. How do you propose doing all that?"

Giskhim walked over to the architect, looked up into his eyes, and addressed him and him alone, again with the aid of Surgal's ready tongue.

"With your kind assistance, Honorable Imhotep."

"Why would I do that?"

"Because it is in your land's best interest. Your land will be the first to suffer the demonic host. Its measure of anguish will be the greatest. More importantly, Honorable Imhotep, I have observed you, and you are more than *just* a man. If you look deeply into my heart, as I have already done with yours, you will better appreciate the absolute necessity of the task before us."

Imhotep, master architect *and* magician, did just that and was greeted by the smiling mental image of a much younger version of the Sumerian, who stood alone, proud and straight, within a glowing fog.

*Is that you Giskhim?*

*Indeed, most Honorable Imhotep, it is I as I feel—a much younger man.*

*How can I justify my assistance in this task? I work at the bidding of my god king, and he is of a certain, steadfast will.*

*That is simple, Honorable One. Explain to your god king this task as a purely architectural exercise, yet something necessary. In the process, you and your workmen will learn much about the workings of the everlasting stone. Besides, it is well-known that there is much yellow gold secreted among the mountains to the south in a land called Kush. Their traders visit my city quite often.*

Imhotep smiled broadly. *Giskhim, you are more shopkeeper than priest.*

*Thank you, Honorable One.* The Sumerian thought with a generous bow. *My father taught me well in the way of things.*

*Indeed, he did,* smirked the Egyptian. *Indeed he did.*

\*   \*   \*

From that day forward, Imhotep conscripted a special cadre of Egyptian surveyors and workmen to build a packed causeway from the river channel to the Western Desert. Giskhim's architect joined them in this undertaking. The same day, a team of stone masons departed downriver for the red granite quarry of everlasting stone located at the river's first cataract. Here also, Giskhim's colleagues accompanied them along with a small expeditionary force, tasked to investigate the rumor of the mountains filled with yellow gold. Then, together, the Egyptian master architect and the Sumerian high priest surveyed the footprint of their future construction. They discussed many forms, but in the end, the pair decided upon one that was enduring—a low rectangle, slope-sided, with a flat roof that diminished the erosion of wind and sand.

\* \* \*

After the passage of three years, Imhotep and Giskhim, now close friends, stood before the completed monument built of everlasting stone—red granite. The Sumerian, now long fluent in the tongue of the Egyptians, conversed directly with Imhotep.

"I and my foremen have learned much from this exercise," the Egyptian admitted.

"How so, my friend?" the Sumerian queried.

"This is my first construction made entirely of such an 'everlasting' material. It has opened my mind to many possibilities for my god king's inner tomb."

Nodding with appreciation, "Indeed, while it is

beautiful, it is a hard stone. But our work here, Imhotep, is not finished."

"How so?" Imhotep said with upraised eyebrows.

"Honorable Imhotep, we have constructed together, with great effort and skill, a mortal structure. Now, we must add its magical defenses."

"What do you have in mind?" the master architect reasonably asked.

"I must commune with the Netherworld's guardian and tell it the meaning of our purpose. I must establish with it an understanding. Meanwhile you, my friend, must add a regeneration spell that will preserve these stones for all eternity. Or, as your people are wont to say, 'for millions of years.'"

Grunting with appreciation for Giskhim's grasp of his language's nuances, Imhotep smirked. *Is there no end to your preparations, Venerable Giskhim?*

*Yes, there is. But the security of our lands is our first concern.*

\* \* \*

Four days before the dire portent was due to take place, the venerable high priest died in his sleep, forever ignorant of whether or not his efforts were in vain. The members of his retinue discovered him in still repose, slack-jawed, and unmoving. Panicked, they called for a physician. Upon arriving, the poor man could do nothing as the priest's body had already become cold. The Sumerians were inconsolable, because in their religion death represented not a glorious new beginning for a life well-lived, but rather a trial of anguish as the soul passed through several phases en route to a hard-earned enlightenment.

Imhotep, also much disturbed by the man's passing, was overheard speaking over the corpse. In truth, the architect prayed for his soul. "Venerable One, who taught me the true measure of one's life, you have gone West without witnessing the final test of your many labors. Your wisdom and conversation will truly be missed, old friend. Good journey! Let nothing forestall your course to paradise. Let nothing harm your *ka*."

Having bid his farewell, the master architect then did a pious thing, something a son would do for his father. He ordered the man's body be prepared for the afterlife in the Egyptian way. This his retinue allowed, as they believed it might somehow aid the journey of the old man's soul.

The next day, three days before the prophecy was to unfold, Imhotep personally surveyed and found a suitable place of burial for the venerable Sumerian. In a cleft overlooking the finished and glistening red monument, Imhotep instructed his master foreman, Saneb, to construct a modest place hidden from prying eyes. This the foreman undertook several days after the portent's passing. Finally, Imhotep personally composed Giskhim's burial inscription, and instructed his master scribe to oversee its excellence in execution.

After the passage of seventy days, when Giskhim's mummy was completed, Imhotep personally saw to his final internment. It was a private ceremony attended by the old man's followers and Imhotep only.

\* \* \*

On the day foretold, the dark master of the Netherworld, the Devourer of Souls, could not contain its ebullience, for it sensed the imminent approach of the seismic disaster. For the first time in its primordial existence, the demon experienced hope that it and its minions might be freed. As for the puny mortal structure, the evil primordial cared not, believing it would fail before them like a crushed eggshell. And with its fall, the Devourer and its kind would be free to invade the Mortal Realm and make it their own— dashing to bits the Creator's carefully laid out plan. Not forgotten, the demon intended to deal with its primordial nemesis, the Guardian of the Netherworld, which ensured the permanence of the Netherworld's boundaries. It too would free the Devourer's wrath.

The seismic event that Giskhim had so accurately foretold was triggered by no terrestrial force. Rather it would be the passage of a dark, supremely dense mass that passed dangerously close to the earth. Fortunately, it careened off the upper atmosphere before continuing on with its celestial wanderings, but not without notice. Just as the moon caused the many tides on a daily basis, this sojourner from deep space did the same, but for one time only. As one might imagine, its near-earth passage affected far more than just the tides. For the asteroid's gravitational pull tore at the upper atmosphere causing spectacular effects, rippled the landscape of the planet, and caused destructive tides. In places, rivers left their courses. By some miracle, the planet's magnetic poles remained in place.

Within Egypt, the rippling of the landscape wreaked havoc upon the Great White Wall of Memphis, the proud fortifications of the capital. These Imhotep would immediately address at the bidding of his king.

Meanwhile at the Sakkaran Plateau, the first two levels of the king's funerary structure shifted, cracked, and in several places failed. Limestone blocks tumbled in a sudden avalanche. This caused the master architect Imhotep to reconsider his plans for his god king's final resting place. The result would be a grand revision and expansion from two to five levels, which would overlook the river valley. As a consequence, Imhotep designed Egypt's first pyramid and King Djoser would be remembered for all time, as would his master architect.

Just west of Sakkara, in a lonely and secluded vale, rocks fell and cracks split along its northern and southern cliffs. Yet, the monument constructed by mere mortals over the Netherworld remained stubbornly steadfast. The structure's massive and everlasting stones budged not one finger's breath as they sealed over the newly-formed rent in the earth. Imhotep's powerful regenerative magic had ensured their soundness.

Meanwhile, far below, their false hopes dashed, the Devourer of Souls and its minions screamed as one in absolute fury and frustration. Meanwhile, the Guardian of the Netherworld just smiled with supreme pleasure.

\* \* \*

The everlasting labors of the ancients would remain unmolested in that desolate and long-forgotten place of shifting sands and weathered rock walls. The twenty Sumerians who participated in its construction grimly knew they would never again see their families nor homeland. This they had discussed beforehand. Those Egyptians who had assisted them were made to understand the need for discretion. These workmen were presented with a choice—either a quick death, or take a terrible oath—after which their tongues were removed. By such extreme artifice the structure lay undisturbed for millennia.

# CHAPTER 1

Four thousand five hundred years later, the dark sojourner rolled, yawed, and tumbled its way back toward the Solar System. Having long ago completed its outbound orbit and the rounding of its apogee, the massive asteroid returned drawn by the gravitation of our star. Little affected its inevitable path. If anything, the gravitation of the massive nickel-iron body constantly added other such objects to its mass.

\*   \*   \*

Their television blared out on the Smithsonian Channel—"Space Archaeologist Uses Satellites to Uncover Ancient Egyptian Ruins." The father and son watched intently. Occasionally they whispered among themselves and took notes. Some four weeks later, they stumbled upon something on Google Earth. What they found was a rectangular object with sides that faced the cardinal points—a promising sign, yet its value remained uncertain.

"Do you think it is a secret military installation? It's not far from Dhashur," the son asked his father.

"Perhaps. But if it was, where are the roads supporting it? Or the barracks for its men?" the father reasoned. "No, my son, this appears to be ancient." He said with a grin, proud of his son's discovery.

Their emotions spiked when they pieced together a handful of meandering artificial traces that wound through the stark desert landscape. The coordinates of the edifice located in the Western Desert, within easily accessibility to the Nile River, and its roadway's valley entrance they eagerly wrote down. The next day the pair set off in their rickety tan Toyota pickup, each with their own dreams of avarice.

Following their GPS device, the audacious grave robbers spotted the gentle saddle where a long-forgotten ancient pavement once exited the desert wastes. Turning off the paved agricultural roadway, they drove up the plateau to the saddle. Stopping, they both appreciated the view that overlooked the entire Sakkaran archaeological preserve at dawn. The first rays transformed the stark white limestone into a rosy red. Having seen their fill, the pair drove on and followed the traces of a sand-filled course for about a kilometer and a half, getting stuck twice in the deep, pumice-like sand before reaching their goal. What they sought lay around a bend in a sandy hollow surrounded by rocky cliffs.

And there it lay. With its western side exposed to the prevailing winds, they slid to a stop next to it. Eagerly each reached into the flatbed to grab their shovels. Sand flew furiously this way and that from the structure's side fronting the ancient pavement. Logically, they thought, that's where they would find an entrance.

As they dug, a slow realization began to form in their minds. What they laid bare was staggering—a massive flat topped structure, perhaps twenty-five meters long by fifteen wide, built of sloped red granite blocks each longer than a train car. Never before had either of them encountered the like.

Then, "I know!" Pant. "The Osireion at Abydos!" the father grunted out while shoveling. "It was constructed of such blocks, but nowhere else in Egypt."

"What about those at Giza?" the son countered. "The ones near the Sphinx? At Khafra's mortuary temple?"

"Much smaller. Smaller by half, if that," his father said. "This construction is so very much like the Osireion."

After several hours of dogged labor they stumbled across a crisp rectangular cutting in the granite facing. Across it, coursing off in both directions, was a hieroglyphic inscription. With spirits buoyed, they dug on to expose the cutting in its entirety. Only then did they go back to their truck for the crowbars. No matter how they tried, the two could not budge the entrance block. With every trick of leverage thwarted, they managed to only break away several large chips from the entranceway's once pristine seam. Tragically for them, that affront was sufficient.

Faced with failure, the pair, frustrated, knew they needed help. That meant sharing their find with the rest of their family—a subject neither wanted to discuss. But there was just one problem. Their truck's front end had settled deeply into the soft sand during their labors, to the point the rear-end tilted toward the sky at nearly a thirty-five degree angle.

Then the son saw the sand move beneath the truck.

"Father! What's that?" the son pointed.

"What's what?" the father said because he hadn't seen the stirring.

"*THAT!*" his son screamed.

*       *       *

That night the father and son failed to return to their village. Their family, much concerned, contacted the local authorities. After a week's worth of searching in ever-widening arcs, the abandoned pickup was finally spotted in the desert by a military helicopter. Half buried in the sand, the vehicle looked like it had been initially swallowed by the desert, and then rudely rejected. Upon landing, the crew found no bodies, no tracks, just smooth trackless sand, and a powered-down smart device attached to the pickup's dash. So they took it in hopes it might provide a clue as to the whereabouts of the missing father and son. None noticed a subtle shifting in the sand beneath the vehicle.

With the device plugged into the helicopter's electrical system, it sprang to life. Google Earth appeared along with a set of GPS coordinates that nearly matched the pickup's location.

Having seen enough, the commander grunted out an order to his squad of six to reconnoiter the surrounding terrain of sand and rock. Holding up the device, Flight Lieutenant Mustafa El Mahdy called out, "The GPS coordinates on this device refer to that stretch of land over there. Fan out and look for any clues."

The six did just that, spreading out in a much-practiced formation, heads down, five meters apart, scanning the surface as if looking for mines. Meanwhile, their commander continued to search through the device, looking for something, *anything*, that might be of value.

The search of the enclosed depression did not take long. Fortunately, no one had returned to the half-buried truck, nor had any ventured near.

"We found two old shovels, sir," he said, holding them up. "Other than that, just a flat-topped rock."

"Oh?" El Mahdy's head snapped up from his attention to the device's cracked screen. "What do you mean by 'a flat-topped rock'?"

"Right over there," the corporal pointed. "Where you said the GPS coordinates pointed."

"Show me." His superior ordered.

Moments later El Mahdy and his observant corporal stood upon a two-by-two meter patch of exposed rock. Getting down on his hands and knees, the lieutenant ran his hand across the remarkably even red granite surface and even put his head down sideways against it. It was near flawless. "This is damn flat soldier. *Too* damn flat." Standing up he checked the smart device once again. The GPS coordinates were spot on. Rubbing his chin in thought, he slowly looked around, and then he saw it—he was standing in the center of a vaguely rectangular outline. Then his instincts kicked in as he got a strange feeling. "Let's get back to the helicopter." It was good they did.

Once airborne, El Mahdy looked down over the depression and saw his confirmation in the helicopter's backwash. "By Allah's beard. There is a rectangular structure down there beneath the sand. Those two grave robbers knew what they were doing." His innate sense of "dread" when standing atop the structure, never verbally expressed, was quickly forgotten with the elation of the discovery below.

Upon returning to his base at Dhashur, the flight lieutenant reported his findings to his superior, who handed off the coordinates to the Egyptian Archaeological Service's office in Sakkara. As the nearest archaeological jurisdiction, the find now became the responsibility and bureaucratic headache of its inspector, Ali Hassan. With his resources stretched to the limit, Hassan already knew who he would contact to investigate this cultural windfall, a man who held his implicit trust, and a good friend, an Austrian Egyptologist named Erik Reissen.

# CHAPTER 2

In the beginning, the Creator sought fit to fashion a place for evil to reside and the souls of the damned to go for their final destruction. This Dark Realm, the antithesis of the Realm of Light and anathema to the Mortal Realm, was devoid of light, love, and hope. Once there, the fallen writhed in desperate agony. A place of pure chaos, dark things scurried and slithered about bedeviling the hopeless with their painful stings and bites. The teasing approach of their chitinous clicks and the abrasive scrape of scales drove the damned mad with fear and dread. So hypersensitized, their mere brush sent a soul shrieking into heart-rending panic.

The master of this frightful realm, the Devourer of Souls, ruled over its denizens and tore apart fallen souls—slowly, awfully. That was its purpose as designed by the Creator, but the primordial was not a dumb construct. Sentient and self-aware, it knew of the other realms of existence and lusted for their souls. It also knew of the weak and easily susceptible ones who inhabited those regions. Upon occasion it communicated with them with promises of power and influence—always for a price. Above all, and contrary to the Divine Plan, the demon wished to breach its boundaries, to reach out, and engulf all of reality. To do so meant the acquisition of power unimagined, not to mention the failure of the Creator's grand design.

To guard against this possibility, the Creator in its infinite wisdom, created another terrible entity. Called by many names, the Guardian of the Netherworld stood by to prevent any demon or dark soul from escaping. Also made sentient and self-aware, this primordial defended its post both against those from within the Dark Realm and from those without.

\*　　\*　　\*

Only once before during its primordial existence had the Devourer of Souls witnessed its maddened dark souls loosed upon the Mortal Realm. The Great Rent of AD 1431, caused by an imbalance between the realms—a vibration, a tremor, tore a hole in the realm's fabric. So the unthinkable had occurred. Because of it, many a dark soul had made passage from the Dark into the Mortal Realm. The Guardian, at first caught unawares, was unable to stop them all. But just before the Devourer could free itself, the Great Rent was slammed shut by the heroic deeds of a mortal, the Lictor of Magic. Enraged beyond any scale of measurement, the dark demon redoubled its plans for revenge and escape, for it had tasted something truly divine—hope.

For all of the Devourer's power and influence, it could not realize its freedom alone. It required mortals of sufficient pliability, who, on its behalf, could somehow breach the Netherworld from their side. Only with their help would those within the Dark Realm become loosed upon the earth.

Indeed, such demented and cruel individuals lived in the Mortal Realm and in Barcelona specifically. Three witches, the sole remnants of a once proud coven, yearned for revenge. Their target and source of white hot hate was the Lictor of Magic, for he and he alone had laid their coven low. The trio yearned for at any price, so the Devourer of Souls selected one of them as a fitting instrument and reached out.

# CHAPTER 3

Portia Le Fey proudly counted her initiation into the Hidden Folk from the year of Our Lord 1018. A girl of only eight seasons, Portia's village, located in a region now known as Tuscany, had been repeatedly raided for provisions by the opposing armies of Byzantium, the Ostrogoths, and the Herulians. Thoroughly ruined by the repeated plundering, its vineyards destroyed, this scenic mountain village's once thriving commerce collapsed. Outright starvation became commonplace. Families disintegrated. More ruin than village, few inhabitants remained within its circuit.

Portia found herself abandoned, emaciated, and nearly feral, when a lone traveler happened upon her. Stooped and walking with a heavy cudgel, the old woman, clothed in coarse flax robes and hood, took pity upon her. When she saw the young girl she stopped, sat down on a roadside curbstone meant for mounting a horse, reached into her robes, and offered the filthy scamp a portion of her bread.

The traveler knew precisely what she was doing. She could see the girl's potential, could feel her strength, her resilience and intellect. Puppy-like, Portia bonded to the woman, who spoke to her with uncommon kindness while not speaking. So began Portia's internship as a witch's apprentice.

In the fullness of time, Portia followed the old Roman patrician and ancient priestess of Cybele far and wide along the paved roads of northern Italy, through its mountainous regions, and beyond into what is now France. Along the way, the once skinny girl filled out, matured, and became an attractive woman and powerful witch in her own right. Her kindly benefactor saw to all of this, openly sharing her hidden wisdom and knowledge, and in the end, even sponsored her passage into the Hidden Folk with her own life. So paid through the time-honored custom of *Wehrgeld*, the young witch took on the status of the old crone, thereby insuring her survival within the Folk. She also adopted her mentor's name, Portia Germanicus Metellus, in tribute to her memory, and added to it her place of birth—*Faesulae*.

*   *   *

One becomes a member of the Hidden Folk in only two ways—by birthright or through an initiation of magical transfiguration. This dichotomy, while a source of strength that can increase their numbers, is also the basis for the vexing and divisive way the Hidden Folk rank themselves. For better or worse, pure bloods tend to hold pride of place whether deserved or not, while those who are "made" must run a formidable gauntlet to earn respect. Survival and longevity however, remain the great equalizers, and are typically how "made" members gain renown within this hidden community. Portia, because of her mentor's sacrifice, avoided much of this clannish nonsense.

While hardly immortal, the Hidden Folk are known to enhance their life spans through a murky process known as rejuvenation—a closely-guarded secret. A popular rumor claimed Sir Charles Darwin was a member. If true, it would explain plenty.

Among their kind are counted sensitives, vampires, werewolves, fey, ghouls, witches, wizards, and *others*. Their lone shared characteristic is being made of flesh and blood, for none of the Hidden Folk are incorporeal—although they are well-known to hold congress with that which is not of the Mortal Realm.

To be counted among the Hidden Folk bestows fierce bonds of loyalty, protection, and hospitality. By their very nature as a close-knit community, considerable advantage presented itself through accumulated wealth, experience, and knowledge.

*   *   *

Sitting on her apartment's balcony festooned with hanging flowers, Portia took in the broad stone square of the *Catedral de la Santa Creu i Santa Eulàlia.* She felt a kinship with the structure, which broke ground in 1298. While not strictly Catholic, the witch went to mass every Sunday to breathe in its scents and luxuriate within its gothic atmosphere of chapels and crypts. She liked it. It was old, venerable, like she was.

This morning, however, while sipping coffee, Portia received a strange tingling sensation. She returned the delicate blue Dresden cup to its matching saucer, placed her hands in her lap, closed her eyes, and concentrated in the warming sun. To any passersby, she appeared to be dozing instead of participating in a telepathic conversation.

*I am the Dark One.* It resonated.

That simple statement's intense power caused Portia's eyes to flutter.

*Dark Sister, successor to Portia Germanicus Metellus, high priestess of Cybele, and senior priestess of your clan, I adjure you to consider my words.*

The witch's heart leapt.

*Oh wise and powerful priestess, I sense your ardent desire to crush an enemy, the Lictor of Magic, for all the foul deeds he has committed against your once strong and proud coven.*

Portia easily saw through the demon's silky words and knew well that there was far more to, and behind, the initiation of this conversation. It *wanted* something. Still, such communication represented an unprecedented opportunity. Perhaps a bargain could be struck that would not forever damn her position.

*Great and powerful Dark One, you recognize well my most heart-felt desire. In truth, I lust to disembowl the Lictor of Magic upon his own sword. But I am too weak to undertake such a task. Is there perhaps something I can do for you? And once accomplished, would you grant me the power to succeed in my fondest desire?*

If the chief demon could have grunted with satisfaction, it would have. Instead, it paused, reflected, and stated, *Dark sister, I grant you all the power that you require.*

With that said, Portia's body began to tremble, not uncontrollably, but with odd purpose—like a tea kettle coming to full boil. When it stopped, she opened her eyes and beheld a new reality. Things were subtly different. Not only did the witch see what occurred, she now sensed why. Below, the tourist with her camera had a taste for gelato and was consciously looking for it. Over there, the restaurant owner fretted over his future receipts. The farmer selling tomatoes and onions from his pushcart frowned with worry about his grandchildren's future. Everywhere she looked, Portia knew what was going to happen. She gasped at the overload, quickly realizing that she would have to master this new ability of anticipating the future.

*So, oh great and powerful Dark One, just what have you granted me?*

**The power to predict where a translocating Lictor of Magic will next go. Master it well.**

*Oh great and powerful Dark One, for this prescience, what now is the reward you seek?*

**The opening of the Netherworld.**

The old witch paused breathlessly to take in fully the magnitude of the task at hand. Much would be required to make it happen. The ramifications stunned her. When she refocused, Portia asked, *Where is this place?*

**In time that will become clear to you.**

*And at that moment, when you and your many dark souls are released, what will become of me and mine?*

**Power and influence unimaginable.**

Hearing that, Portia gasped in anticipation. Visions of a dead Lictor of Magic filled her head along with a Vatican reduced to tattered ruins, its *pontifex maximus* discredited, and Barcelona as the religious center of a revived pagan theocracy.

# CHAPTER 4

A middle-aged US Air Force technician sat in his station before three flat screens. Located deep within a mountain located near Colorado Springs, Colorado, his windowless niche was illuminated with soft, shadow-resistant lighting that mimicked the real thing. Only the institutional wall clock hinted at the correct local time. During the winter holidays, he enjoyed tracking Santa Claus and answering emails from nerdy kids about the jolly man's progress. This morning however, or was it afternoon, Master Sergeant Gene Roberts had a lot on his mind.

The flat screen to his right was dominated by his MSWord email. At present, a message from Mauna Kea, Hawaii stood open, its contents revealed. The screen to his left displayed his USAF Space Command link. The last flat screen, the one front and center, displayed two side-by-side images that frightened the master sergeant to his core. One was a predicted "near-Earth" orbital plot. The other a deep space radio image of a massive asteroid that the Very Long Base Array

(VLBA) constructed from its ten radio telescope installations scattered across the US and its territories.

"So what do you think, master sergeant?" Lieutenant Josh Myers, the whiz-kid Vanderbilt physics grad asked as he peeked over the man's shoulder.

"Very scary, sir. Before we send this telemetry up the ladder, I would strongly suggest that we get Arecibo, Green Bank, and the Very Large Array (VLA) in on the party."

"Agreed. Let 'em fry that big boy until it glows."

Roberts nodded, picked up the landline receiver, and got the ball rolling.

*     *     *

Discovery can be pure serendipity, like the time a sloppy researcher sneezed into an open petrie dish killing a dangerous bacteria. But more often than not, discovery is the result of dogged effort. Dr. Paula Rohr earned her pride of place early on from leaning into a telescope's eye piece until she had blackened the orbits of her blood-shot eyes. With the advent of digital imagery, her beautiful browns no longer endangered by a prankster's oily smudges or accidental bruises.

Rohr grew up in central Germany as a precocious

and inquisitive only child. Daughter of a father who owned an Audi dealership, when she came of age, Paula never wanted for a car. Her mother Gretchen was a biology lecturer in her hometown's university prep school. While her father brought home the bacon, Paula's mother encouraged her that she could to do anything, if she put her will to it.

Blessed with an empirical mind, a talent for mathematics, and a love for *Star Wars*, it was no surprise to anyone that Paula's majored in astronomy at the university in Bonn. With high grades throughout, she liked to hang out at the Effelsberg radio telescope that was operated by the Max Planck Institute for Radio Astronomy. With nearly half the observation time at the telescope available to qualified individuals, Rohr pressed her astronomy professor and got her chance early in her coursework to peer deeply into the cosmos. She, was, *hooked*.

Six years later, and now with a PhD in hand, Rohr showed promise and became the youngest research radio astronomy assistant at the institute. Four months into her first year, Paula detected something that no one else did. It was a dark body moving incredibly fast toward the Solar System. The object received through an academically arcane system the provisional name of

2008 RQ36, which indicated the year of its discovery and that it was one of many objects identified in that year. Three months later, Paula had amassed sixteen independently confirmed observations from other astronomers—sufficient to plot a tentative trajectory, which earned for the object an official number granted by the International Astronomical Union—(417001) 2008 RQ36. According to the plot data, without question the object's orbital history was a long, oblique one, which suggested to Rohr a possible near-Earth encounter back in antiquity.

How close?

Rohr ran the object's projected trajectory several times. Each time her object came dangerously close to the Earth's orbital path with a gravitational keyhole, or plantary attraction, of only thirty-one miles or fifty kilometers. In other words, Rohr's calculations had the near-Earth asteroid skirting past the planet at the mid-boundary layer of the planet's atmosphere.

Too damn close was the answer.

Ten years later, the German astronomer's plot estimation had not appreciably changed. An impact was in the cards as much as a close brush. On top of that, the most recent radio imagery of (417001) 2008 RQ36 placed its mass at an enormous 2.9 trillion kilograms, with a radius of over three kilometers. While big, the asteroid was nowhere as big as a planetoid. Given its remarkable speed and the density of its radar echo, (417001) 2008 RQ36 was determined to be an iron-nickel body complete with its own gravity. At this point, Rohr decided to name the body, Gravitron—after a favorite carnival ride from her youth.

On the international Torino Scale, an accepted international method to describe the flyby and impact effects of near-Earth objects, Gravitron was rated at either a seven or a ten. The Torino rating of seven connoted the worse-case scenario of a near-miss,

> A very close encounter by a large object, which ... poses an unprecedented but still uncertain threat of a global catastrophe ... International contingency planning is warranted.

while the Torino rating of ten was for a direct impact.

> A collision is certain, capable of causing global climatic catastrophe that may threaten the future of civilization as we know it, whether impacting land or ocean.

As of the Mauna Kea email, Gravitron's much hoped for near-Earth flyby, was scheduled to occur in eighteen months.

*    *    *

Two days later, the President of the United States was briefed on Gravitron's near-Earth approach and its implications, by his National Science Advisor, Dr. Georgia Shinto. At the conclusion of her concise three-minute slide presentation in the Oval Office, the president frowned, rubbed his chin, and remarked, "Well, from what you just told me, either all life on the planet is going away, or, those who survive will really have their hands full. Is that correct, doctor?"

"Yes, Mr. President," the diminutive middle-aged Asian said, "an impact will claim us all, pure and simple. Whereas a close flyby will tear away a portion of our atmosphere and rearrange our planet's surface."

"Jesus. Is there anything we can do to redirect the course of this asteroid?"

"Perhaps, Mr. President. Might I suggest you ask the Joint Chiefs about that, and in particular the US Air Force and their Space Command division. They may have some ideas."

The president scribbled down a note.

"But there may be another avenue to pursue, Mr. President, one that is ... rather unconventional."

"Well, Dr. Shinto, let's not play games. What's this other option?"

"It's called The International Integrated Interface Society, sir. They are called TIIIS for short."

"Never heard of them. Who are they?"

"Perhaps the most powerful paranormal organization on the planet, that is, besides the Vatican."

The president sat back and stared at his national science advisor in complete disbelief. "Okay doctor, if you're serious, now you have my attention." The president said folding his hands before him. "What can TIIIS do about this kamakazi asteroid that Space Command can't?"

"With your permission sir, I would like to arrange a brief meeting between you and their president. She can explain their capabilities far better than I."

After a brief pause for thought, the president looked up and said, "Do it doctor. I'll give her three minutes."

*   *   *

Georgia Shinto and Betsy Silver Moon were friends since their college days at Northwestern University. While it had been awhile, the sound and energy of Shinto's voice on the telephone told the extreme sensitive far more than did the science advisor's initial words.

"Betsy, this is Georgia Shinto ..."

"What's the crisis Georgia?"

"No time for pleasantries old friend?"

"Not when you call me out-of-the-blue. So spill it."

"Damn. You're still so witchy. Do you know what a NEO is?"

After a brief pause, "You mean a near-Earth object?"

"Precisely. One's arriving in eighteen months and it'll be a real doozy. The president is handing off this one to the Joint Chiefs, but I got you a three-minute interview with him to explain what TIIIS can do. I told the president TIIIS could make a real difference. What do you say, Bets? Up for briefing the President of the United States?"

"Send me the particulars Georgia. You still have my email?"

"Yes, I do. Is it encrypted?"

"Of course it is. Now, how's life my good friend?"

*   *   *

During the flight from San Antonio to Washington, DC, in the TIIIS flat black corporate jet, the president thought long and hard on how to best communicate her message to the president. Well-known for his instinctive, crisp, hard-hitting, and no-nonsense demeanor, Silver Moon knew she could be painfully direct. Given her narrow three-minute window, Silver Moon also recognized how to best pass on her message, but as for its content, she concluded imagery would be the best.

A massively armored White House limo picked up the short-statured Native American from Dulles. With doors nearly a foot thick, when they closed, all sound disappeared. Dressed in a tailored dark-blue business suit and skirt with a simple, scoop-collared white blouse, Silver Moon looked the part, but felt like an outsider on her way to the principal's office.

The ride itself passed all too quickly as she sat cocooned in heavily-padded black leather. Having left her purse back in the plane, all Silver Moon carried in her jacket side pocket was a New Mexico driver's license and passport. As the sensitive expected, both got a rigorous once-over several times before she was allowed to exit the vehicle and enter the East Wing. IDs in hand, she passed through a metal detector followed by a body scanner, both indignities created by modern-day terrorism and society's lack of respect.

The walk to the Oval Office seemed like a brief but surreal visit to an art museum, with paintings here and busts there of America's many historic personages and close allies. Her clicking short heels transitioned from marble to carpeting, and then, quite suddenly, her armed guard stopped, and rapped twice on an oddly curved door that blended beautifully into the wall. Listening to his earpiece, the man nodded, and opened it.

\*　　\*　　\*

The sheer weight of a nation's responsibility pressed against Silver Moon's mind like altitude-plugged ears. Still seated, the president raised his right index finger to signal a moment. When finished, he returned the receiver to its cradle, stood, and rounded the corner of the Resolute desk.

Two things impressed the Native American—how cramped the Oval Office seemed, and how tall the president was.

Extending her hand, once they made contact the president of TIIIS smiled and telepathically broadcasted directly to the president, *Mr. President, I am here to offer you an alternative to planetary catastrophe and global EMP devastation.*

To her surprise, the president smiled back, held her hand for two beats longer than necessary, and responded, *I don't doubt it for a moment. So Madam President, what's the plan?*

\* \* \*

Five minutes later Silver Moon again sat in a White House limo, but it wasn't going back to Dulles, but rather to the Pentagon where she was to attend a flash meeting with the Joint Chiefs of Staff. During that ten minute drive, Silver Moon reviewed her impressions. Before she finished with her meeting, the president had called the Pentagon to gather the Joint Chiefs together—hence the reason for her change of itinerary. Things were happening very fast and that surprised her. After all, Washington wasn't supposed to be so agile. *Note to self.*

As for the president himself, a highly-complex man whom she did not vote for, overall she left deeply impressed, calmed, and yet very concerned for his welfare and that of his family. Above all, Silver Moon had not expected how telepathically sensitive the president was. That fact explained a lot, to the point she actually extended him an invitation to join TLIS.

She had smiled at his easy response, *I'll think*

*about it once I'm out of this mad house.*

\*   \*   \*

By the time Silver Moon arrived at the Pentagon, the security protocol felt like old hat. But much unlike the White House, the austere sameness of the Pentagon screamed pure bureaucracy. Again led by an armed guide through a maze of near-identical rings, corridors, and levels, she finally arrived before a door that was opened for her. Within was a simple conference table surrounded by seven uniformed men who represented the nation's many services.

Hectic curiosity assaulted her, mixed with frustration. One of the seven the Navajo sensed, was openly hostile. Glancing about, she sat at the conference table's end chair nearest the door and noted with dark humor that it did not have shackles. She estimated that well over one hundred years of military experience was arrayed before her. All sat erect, well turned out, and wore deadly serious faces. *They're all poker players*, she realized.

"Welcome, President Silver Moon," the chairman smoothly began with a nod of acknowledgment. "Why are we here today?"

"I am here to get the telemetry data on a rogue

near-Earth asteroid that wants to destroy our planet." Silver Moon stated evenly.

"And why, madam, do you want that information?" the Navy admiral asked pointedly. So Silver Moon did what was natural, she firmly took command and her voice rang with it, along with a touch of encouraging magic.

Turning to the admiral and looking him dead in the eye, "That, sir, is classified. But I'm willing to potentially sacrifice twenty of my best people to save the planet."

Breaking away, she then directly addressed the other end of the conference table. "Mr. Chairman, what I need from this august body are: one," as she ticked off her fingers, "the precise plot of the asteroid's path within one AU at perihelion; two, precisely the duration of its passage and when it will occur; and three, precisely where over the planet the asteroid's shadow will fall."

The seven sat there for several moments like obedient students who had just received their homework assignments. When Silver Moon allowed the spell to break, all knew what they had to provide.

"Mr. Chairman, here is my card," as she passed it to the Marine general immediately to her right. He glanced at it, looked quizzically back at her, and passed it on.

"I need that telemetry in two days' time. My email, by the way, is fully encrypted."

Silver Moon then pushed her chair back and stood. "Gentlemen, thank you for your valuable time."

As soon as the conference room's door closed, the chairman glanced at the wall clock. Only three minutes had passed.

The Navy admiral murmured what all seven were privately thinking, "What a firecracker!"

# CHAPTER 5

Nestled within an oak forest in southwestern Pennsylvania, stands the Old Oaks Academy—the intellectual hub of a paranormal organization called The International Integrated Interface Society. The start of the fall semester always seemed to energize the sun-dappled campus with fresh faces, full of enthusiasm, and instructors, full of hope. With course schedules, maps in hand, and carrying overloaded backpacks, students hurried here and there like so many ants.

In one building, Old Main, a tall, broad-shouldered instructor wearing a tweed sports coat and tie, stood patiently behind his podium as several late stragglers slipped into the remaining seats. The lecture hall's wooden floors and benches however, creaked and groaned loudly, effectively announcing their tardy arrival. Noting this from beneath his heavy blond eyebrows, his roster count now complete, the instructor began.

"Welcome to Demonology 101. I am Mr. Stone, your instructor. Study the syllabus before you carefully.

Thoroughly read and commit to memory everything on your thumb drive—specifically *The Knot of Eternity* and its commentary. Their collective wisdom just might save your life someday—as they did mine, several times."

These terse instructions caused heads to rise, several to pick up and examine their tiny storage devices, and one to whisper behind his hand to his neighbor, "Is this guy for real?"

Stone's heightened senses easily overheard this exchange, "I am dead serious, Mr. Grant." Stone said with finality. "If you're not, then I suggest that you get yourself out of this business. This isn't Hogworts. And to emphasize this fact Mr. Grant, let's make this a teachable moment."

Stone purposely shifted to his former military command presence with his hands behind his back. "When next we meet, you, sir, will deliver a two-minute presentation on the significance of this campus' chapel memorial. Is that clear mister?"

The wide-eyed Grant made a quick nod. His deep red blush was sufficient for Stone. As for the rest of those in attendance, he saw a noticeable improvement in their posture and attention. He then continued.

"There will be five quizzes, a midterm, and final examination. Of the five quizzes, your three best efforts will be recorded. All quizzes and tests will occur here in this auditorium, and will be handwritten in blue books with Number Two pencils that I will provide. Absence for any reason from either the midterm or final will result in a failure for this course. I will not tolerate cheating of any kind. It will result in immediate failure for this course."

The heavily tanned and fit instructor, who stood ramrod straight before his audience of forty-five, took in all the open mouths, and brazenly met each of their stares with his cool blue eyes. Stone's high and tight blond haircut spoke subliminal volumes. Thoroughly pleased that he had gotten their undivided attention, the native of north Texas moved on.

"Are there any questions?" Allowing for a short pause, "Seeing none, let's begin," he said as he leaned in heavily upon his podium.

"Demonology, ladies and gentlemen, is serious business. Preparing for it, is serious business. Any half-hearted, flakey approach to the subject can prove fatal—or worse. Remember that. There are worse things than death."

A tentative hand raised. It was attached to a bookish-looking young man with horn-rimmed glasses.

"Ah, Mr. Stone. Are you the same dude who survived the Contest in the Aralkum Desert?"

Stone read his mind. "Yes, Mr. Weathersby, I am."

"Holy shit!" the awed student murmured. "So you're the one ..."

Then Stone grinned back at the student. "Mr. Weathersby, I can assure you my shit is anything but holy."

\*   \*   \*

Later that afternoon, elsewhere on campus, the same instructor became the student. He lay spread-eagled on his stomach behind a rifle with a thick extension added to its already long barrel. Fortunately, the rifle's bipod helped considerably. With his right eye planted against the rifle's telescopic sight, the student listened to his instructor's smooth and patient voice, who sat cross-legged next to him.

Gunny Butch Grainger peered through the lens of a high-powered observation scope at the target in question. His mop of graying red hair threatened to cover his ears from beneath his reversed ball cap. A pair of earmuffs encircled his neck, unused because of the huge suppressor. The native big game hunter of Big Sky country continued on with his patient and silky smooth commentary—so unlike Ian Crosby's exotic South African accent—a man who had died protecting his Lictor at the Contest in the Desert.

"Okay, Mr. Stone, let's remember why we're here. The bad guys are beyond your Bone Sword's deadly reach, beyond your favorite handgun's range. Still, it's time to 'reach out and touch *something.*' So we're training with modified ammo I cooked up to simulate the ballistic characteristics of a composite silver-lead round. Always keep in mind the constraints of what you are working with."

The man paused to rub his eyes. Then he returned to his lens.

"Alright, Mr. Stone, this time breathe normally until you capture your target. Then, just before you fire, hold your breath for one count, settle yourself, exhale, and gently apply pressure to the trigger. Do not squeeze or jerk it."

*Cough* sounded the report of the heavily suppressed rifle. Shortly followed by the ringing *Ting* of the distant target's metal backing plate.

Grainger commented, "Not bad, Mr. Stone. Not bad at all. Surely a fatal shot, but I know you can do better. This time, consider again the effect of the windage on a lighter round."

*Cough.*

"Much better. Sweet group. Now, quickly acquire the three hundred yard target and fire when ready."

Moments later, *Cough.*

"Windage, Mr. Stone. Don't forget your windage."

\*     \*     \*

Across campus an attractive woman wrapped up her intermediate-level class in spell casting. Olive-skinned, with a triangular face and narrow long nose, her shiny jet black hair surrounded her face like two raven's wings. She mixed up with the old "tried and trues," a practical handful from her family's own spell collection. The Alexandrian Egyptian believed in such variety. Her entire point was to emphasize the daily practicality of useful magic in direct counterpoint to the portrayed popular notion that all magic had to be dark and dangerous. Spell casting was a teachable, learnable skill, even for normals with zero sensitivity.

Well-known on campus for her infectious smile and generous personality, Dr. Melaina Makris nonetheless pushed her students to achieve that which they considered impossible. Her typical demonstrations took place outside of the classroom, in this case the campus parking lot. The lightly-built five-foot something posed the following challenge.

"Imagine yourself in an urban parking structure. Its near midnight and you discover one of your tires is as flat as a pancake. What do you do? Go through all the trouble of physically changing the tire? Or, do you cast a spell to temporarily plug and inflate it?"

"Chew on that. Read up on Spells Fourteen and Thirty. They should give you hints galore as to how to fix a tire."

The eight students clustered around her, heads down took furious notes on their pads.

"How cool," one murmured.

"Now, imagine yourself in an emergency situation. For whatever reason, a vehicle needs to be moved aside to make way. What do you do? Call 911 and wait for the trapped victim to bleed out and expire? Or, do you cast a spell to temporarily provide yourself with increased strength?"

Dr. Makris walked over to a large GMC truck. En route, her long and artistic fingers made several spidery motions. Pursing her full lips in preparation for exertion, the witch lifted the rear-end of the vehicle by its bumper overhead. Dropping it, the truck bounced and rebounded like a toy on its oversized shocks and wheels.

"The only problem with Spell Fifty-Two is you might later need a chiropractor, so don't overdo it."

Smiles and more notetaking.

As Dr. Makris lead her gaggle back to their classroom, she felt a warm tingling on her consciousness. Abruptly stopping and turning around to face her students, Dr. Makris slammed her mental blocks down like a spiked portcullis gate. Only one of the students reacted as if slapped in the face. Makris confronted the bold young woman with blond hair and looked her in the eye.

"Ms. Baker, are you aware you can be expelled for an unauthorized telepathic intrusion?"

"I, ah ... didn't mean ..."

"Did you not sign this institution's *Rules and Regulations*?"

"I, yeah, I suppose so."

"You didn't read it, did you."

"I, ah, no I didn't."

The exasperated witch then asked, "So what was so vital that you were willing to jeopardize your station within this institution?"

"Well, ah, aren't you married to Mr. Stone?"

The Alexandrian witch gaped at the student. "Why would you pose such a personal question?"

"Ah, campus scuttlebutt says you are."

"Ms. Baker, do you believe everything you hear?" The Egyptian witch's once kind brown eyes now turned obsidian black with palpable outrage.

"Well, well ... it's just he's so hot," the millennial threw out with a causal flick of her hand.

*So that's it.* "That, Ms. Baker, I well know," Dr. Makris smiled knowingly as she turned on her heel.

*This generation has no sense of boundaries.*

\*     \*     \*

Half a world away, this time within Vatican City, another presentation had taken place earlier that very day.

"The world is an extremely dangerous place, filled with many monstrous *things,*" the wizened and diminutive nun began. She wore a black habit and stiffly starched cowling that cruelly creased her chin. Her ruddy face and cheeks were dominated by a left eye entirely whitened by a cataract; her right glittered like an icy blue jewel. In another time, such a countenance would have marked her as a witch, which of course, she was.

"Our colleagues in the Brotherhood of St. Paul are famously tasked with conducting the exorcisms of pernicious demons, and hunting down those who conjure them. Their operations, consequently," she shrugged, "get all the hype—the many movies and books written about them. We, however," she pointed to herself and gestured expansively to her audience, "members of Pro Deo, are tasked with addressing the relatively mundane—the many *things* that should not be known, much less used. *These things,*" her index finger pointed up, "that can do far worse than kill you."

She scanned the sober and frightened faces before her for a second time. It was a big recruitment class with five Africans, two Asians, and five Europeans. The times were fast becoming tenuous. Contrary to Vatican expectations, the "relatively mundane" had become a serious problem. The sister worried about that and the innate ability of her charges to deal with them. Unconsciously, she scanned their auras, calculated their worth, and estimated their sheer ability to survive. What she saw was not promising.

One, however, unlike the rest, had remained at peace, confident during her practiced tirade. She saw he listened and appreciated her each and every word with eyes that spoke of hard-earned experience. Sister Mary

Gabriella, all four foot eleven, descended the wooden steps from her lectern and approached the fit and tanned man with black hair and clear green eyes. She dared to reach out and lightly clasped his folded hands with hers, of parchment white skin. The contrast was striking. She noted with pleasure that he had not flinched at her approach or touch. She gazed deeply into those sparkling eyes.

"You are indeed a nervy one," Sister Gabriella assessed then. "And you have seen much that few could imagine."

The man simply nodded and she removed her hands, rubbing them together as if trying to warm them, but in actual fact, they had been numbed senseless upon contact. "Sister Josephina Busby has informed me of your case, and of your potential, *Herr* Dr. Reissen. Here, however, you will have much to prove." She turned abruptly away, sending her black robes, trailing headpiece, beads, and crucifix cork-screwing, as she returned to stand behind the raised lectern.

"When next we meet in two days' time," she announced, "you will have read the first three chapters of *The Knot of Eternity*, which is on the thumb drive provided. You will find a translation of that text in your native tongue. Return prepared to discuss those chapters and provide an assessment of the book's author. Every author has their biases. Find this one's. That is all for today. You are dismissed."

*   *   *

Later that day, Sister Gabriella cornered Sister Josephina Busby in a convent hallway. "Sister, a word, if you please," Sister Gabriella asked her much younger and fiery red-headed colleague. "Do you have any inkling of how powerful Dr. Reissen's aura is? Or for that matter, where within the *Schemata* his abilities may lay?"

Looking down to hide her smile before answering, Sister Josephina Busby, Egyptologist, and expert in that culture's many religious and magical practices, said, "His dossier is quite complete, sister. Haven't you read it?"

"Yes, I have," she said with a dismissive wave, "but there are dossiers, and then there are *the* documents, which—let us just say, can be massaged and edited. I prefer a straightforward conversation between individuals to ascertain the *truth* of a matter."

"So you believe me to be a source of truth?" Sister Josephina countered, slightly amused.

"Indeed I do, you impudent youngster," she said with a snap of her blue eye. "So what is your opinion of Dr. Reissen?"

Sister Josephina paused, gathered her tumultuous thoughts, and said, "It is true his teal to cobalt blue aura can be quite intense, especially when his emotions spike, which blessedly is not often. But as to his innate paranormal abilities, he is the only child of two extreme sensitives. They were interviewed by our society when Erik first applied to the Pontifical College for his research grant. At that time, they were informally ranked somewhere between seven or eight on the *Schemata*."

"Hidden Folk?" the elderly nun naturally assumed given the high psychic levels.

"No, nothing like that. Just extremely gifted normals."

"Hmm," the old nun murmured.

"As to what level Erik's, excuse me, Dr. Reissen's may be, is anyone's guess. Given the *Schemata* tops out at nine, of course he may eventually become an unclassified, given sufficient training, practice, and experience in the field."

"And how well do you know Dr. Reissen?" the old nun probed, with both eyes squinting.

"He's a sound scholar and good colleague."

"Just that sister?"

"And he is a dear friend. We studied together at the Pontifical College. In a tight situation, I know he would cover my back."

"I see. Do you see him as a warrior perhaps?"

"I know that he has done his stint in the Austrian military, if that is what you mean."

Sister Gabriella breathed, "Fascinating."

"How so?"

"Your friend Erik may be just what our society has been looking for—a hybrid."

"Hybrid?"

"Someone who can successfully bridge the gap between the Brotherhood of St. Paul, and us."

"Is that even possible?" Sister Josephina said with mild surprise.

"Officially, no. But practically speaking, perhaps. By the way, when I touched Dr. Reissen, we grounded each other."

"Really?"

"Yes. Even now, he is powerful in ways he cannot imagine. He has great potential."

# CHAPTER 6

Reissen arranged for the six month sabbatical from his duties as Professor of Egyptology and Archaeology at the University of Vienna. After his superb management of the excavation and publication of the magician Djedi's tomb, his departmental chairman could not refuse him. Besides that frenetic experience had worn poorly on him.

So when his friend and colleague Sister Josephina Busby of the Vatican approached Reissen to consider another option, perhaps a new career within the secretive Pro Deo society, the archaeologist jumped at it. Soon afterward, the process began with a long conversation with a certain Cardinal Guillermo Alberti. He informed the Egyptologist that a six month probationary period would be necessary in order to assess his fitness, before he would be allowed to continue his training as an actual member of the society. Reissen took the offer.

From that day forward, Reissen's quarters within the Vatican amounted to a sparsely furnished monk's cell with communal facilities at the end of the hallway. On the plus side, the Spartan atmosphere suited Reissen as it provided few distractions while he applied himself to his introductory classes in thaumaturgy, metaphysics, and demonology.

As the archaeologist sat with his laptop open beneath his lone, dusty postage stamp of a window, he reflected to never again grouse about the crampedness of his Vienna departmental office nor its multiple, panoramic flat screens.

He leaned into his chair with a creak and pulled up his assignment, *The Knot of Eternity*. The first thing Reissen noted was the text was a translation by someone named G.L. Love, which was edited in 1960 by another named T. Good. He found their surnames odd and considered them to be *nom du plumes*. As it was, neither name rang a bell, so he initiated an Internet search and found out Love was indeed a Love and a Hellenistic scholar to boot, who flourished during the early twentieth century. Good had been one of his students. Reissen concluded: *two Classical philologists, most likely specialists in* koiné *Greek. That makes the author of* The Knot of Eternity *ancient, and most likely of Alexandrian origin—somewhere between the fourth century BC through fourth century of our era. But can I do better and narrow that down?*

Reissen saw that the Greek text of the original was also on his thumb drive. He began his analysis and realized an important fact. The word for "knot," specified in the Greek text, happened to be one of those words whose meaning shifted widely depending upon context. In fact, Reissen thought Love's translation of "knot" was a bit of a stretch as it could have meant just as easily "burl," "kink," "node," and "nodus," along with "knot." That suggested to the Austrian the book's Greek title itself was a strangled translation from some other language, which given the express purpose of the Alexandrian Library—to translate all the world's written works, made sense.

So which language? Reissen gambled on something Egyptian, Near Eastern, or West Asian, because the Alexandrian Library's contents held such literary works other than those in Greek and Latin. He then settled on, as a working hypothesis, the original work predating the Alexandrian period, sometime *before* the fourth century BC. With this train of thought in mind, the archaeologist began to read Sister Gabriella's assignment.

## The First Lesson

From somewhere deep within the vast void of the earliest Universe, the Creator smiled as the grand plan went into motion. For out of that abysmal darkness, it created light and matter. From those constituent parts the realms of existence came into being along with their various guardians and overseers. Then, with great care and deliberation, the Creator caused its greatest creation: the First and Second Souls.

The First Soul, a construct fashioned with free will, was tasked with the overriding desire to preserve and protect that which the Creator created. The First Soul, afforded with many protections, evolved through incarnation, but was not allowed to attain perfection and ultimate transcendence. For to do so would remove it from its primary task–the preservation and protection of the Cosmic Order.

Reissen grunted. *This is a totally pagan cosmology, filled with cosmic dualism. That makes its origin most likely Zoroastrian or even pre-Zoroastrian in date. If so, that would potentially push this document's authorship back to the first millennium, or even older.*

The archaeologist then went to the passage's commentary by Good and found his confirmation.

What may seem to us as irreconcilable, the old ones took as complementary, and thus as confirmation of the manifold powers of the gods. Although ancient logic is not ours, it has its own consistency and integrity. Consequently, one must leave behind the world of rational and scientific causality in order to gain entrance to the world of magic.

Reissen's empirical side, however, balked as he read and reread the words of that final sentence. Such a bold and matter-of-fact manifesto challenged his personal underpinnings, in spite of his deep familiarity and understanding of the magical Egyptian *Pyramid Texts*. But before that revelation fully took held, he recognized something else. *The Knot of Eternity* represented a dangerous voice, a heretical alternative if not an outright threat to the authoritative tenets of Judaism, Christianity, and Islam. But on the other hand, such a perspective provided an opening to a brand new world, one hoary with age, backed by the experience of generations of sensitives.

# CHAPTER 7

Few could appreciate just how "special" the Barcelona coven was. Established formally at the end of the first century BC as a frontier chapter of the Rome-based *Consilium magorum et sagarum*—The Council of Magicians and Witches, it remained staunchly primitive and pagan, with roots that went back thousands of years. Some insiders speculated that the Neolithic shamans of the region were the source of the coven's ultimate germ. This nicely explained the enclave's well-known, if not outright barbarism. Blessed with a large number of high but dark adepts, many were considered "assisted," or "boosted," by extremely dark entities.

By the end of the European Enlightenment, the coven's long recognized antics had become for CMES more of a curse than a blessing. In 1870, CMES, for the first time in the organization's five millennia long history, banished the lawless coven from its membership rolls, and in the process, removed its protection—all due to their excessive practices. Then, in the summer of 2015, their collective karma finally caught up with them.

*    *    *

On that warm star-crossed night, the hunter smelled the heavy copper reek of the Barcelona coven's plight from halfway across the city. Rushing as quickly as it could, it arrived just before the police to take in the unimaginable bounty of delicious resources.

The blood of sixty-two victims soaked deeply into the cracks of the neighborhood restaurant's sidewalk pavers. When saturated, it pooled, and freely flowed into the street gutters. But as the hunter neared, it detected a scent of something sharp and sour, the unfortunate taint of poisonous silver.

*So many high adepts slaughtered this way. So many ruined livers that I cannot harvest! What a waste!* The frustrated entity screamed in its mind, as it hurriedly glanced about frustrated, still trying to fully grasp the magnitude of the loss.

When the hunter stopped at the gory edge of the circle, it took stock of the sight, and arrived at a frightening thought. *Who did this? Who could pack this coven into such a tight space?*

Then it noticed a common theme—the vast majority of the still weeping, deep wounds, were delivered horizontally, with considerable force and power. Torsos were cleaved in two. Heads rolled. The image of a helicopter's rotating blades came to mind.

Now walking around the border of the gruesome scene, it noted the pattern was consistent and concluded that someone or thing had hacked their way around, encircling the coven. *Forcing them together into a tight defensive formation, just like a border collie herding sheep. Sheep! No one would dare call this coven a herd of sheep. Yet, something had truly frightened them so.*

The encirclement ended in the center, where three remained, staggered together, leaning back-to-back, tripod-like and upright, all without their heads. The hunter recognized who they were in spite of their condition. *Who did this?* It again asked.

Looking beyond the bloody circle, there lay clear evidence of attempted retaliation, and finally, frantic panic. Magically blasted trees were strewn about, fragmented into shards of spindled wood. Here, torn up roadway. There, deeply-gouged furrows into the sidewalk's pavers. A crushed-in car had the misfortune to park nearby, smashed like a soda can. *Their powerful bolts had all missed their attacker ... somehow.*

Standing with hands on hips in wonderment and more than a little confusion, it again asked, *What could do this to sixty-two coven adepts?*

From afar, it heard the blaring cadence of nearing police klaxons. It was time to go. There was nothing here of value to harvest. Besides, humans were gathering about, drawn in by their traditionally odd mixture of horror and fascination. Their curiosity sickened the dhampirica as it turned to leave in utter disgust.

*What a waste!*

# CHAPTER 8

The Barcelona sun baked the town square's cobblestones where a noisy tour guide shepherded his flock by the worn steps of a twelfth century cathedral. Nearby, under a tasseled gold and maroon striped café awning, three elegant-looking women huddled close in conversation over their coffees. Rich and creamy aromas filled the air. A glance from a passerby would not be able to place their decade, but that would be understandable.

The youngest of the three had just turned three hundred and nineteen, while the elder of this tight clutch of was well over a thousand. All were Hidden Folk, in most regards outliers and separate from humanity, but who chose to walk among them unseen and undetected. Some of their kind even *hunted* and *feasted* upon humanity.

"Barcelona has not been the same since the Racó de la Vila massacre of '15," said the first in reference to the sudden loss of sixty-two colleagues in one evening. "Our enclave, somehow, must recover."

"Recover," snorted the second, "there are only three of us left! And that's only because of a flat tire that caused our tardiness."

The third simply nodded.

"I say we seek *revenge*," said the first with a tight fist.

"Oh yes, by all means, but revenge against whom?" retorted the second. "Proper revenge requires a hard target."

The third piped up, "I know who did it."

"Well," said the first, "who did it then?"

"TIIIS."

"Them? Do you really believe that?" the second asked with a dismissive wave. "Those nincompoops can't fight their way out of a wet paper bag. And besides, who in their right mind would call themselves The International Integrated Interface Society? What kind of name is that? Some startup from Silicon Valley?"

"It indeed was TIIIS," the third said with unequivocal finality. "They became emboldened after their champion's victory in the Aralkum Desert. Defeating three of our champions was an impressive feat by anyone's standards."

"He *cheated*," the second said. "He could translocate. No one knew that. Our champions didn't have a prayer."

"Again, by my reckoning, three against one was not a fair bargain either," The third pointed out. "Besides, all three of our *champions* were not even chosen from our own. They were all contract operators."

Ignoring the third's last observation, the first demanded. "Where do you think their champion learned such an arcane ability?"

"He was tutored by a brood mistress of the *Argenti*." The third softly provided.

"You're jesting," the first scoffed.

"No, I am not," the third maintained.

"Those *rodents* don't share anything with anybody," the first sneered, "much less their abilities to translocate."

"They did," the third firmly countered. "Furthermore, I read the blood pools of our fallen kin after that massacre. All were stained with silver. Only one could have done so, their champion, their Lictor of Magic."

At that pronouncement by the elder and long-time mentor of the other two, the three witches bowed as one to sip their coffees. From across the square, that action looked more than vaguely birdlike.

"So our target is the translocating TIIIS Lictor of Magic, who wields a silver sword? Now that will be a tall order," said the first with widened eyes for emphasis.

"Agreed," said a glum and deflated second.

The third, deep in thought, said nothing for several moments. Then, just as she was about to say something, she halted with eyes like saucers. She grasped firmly on the edge of the wrought iron tabletop and exclaimed, "Oh my, someone has attempted to tamper with the Gate of the Netherworld! And, and, they have died. Two ... horribly." She took in a quick breath to add. "Such rank ignorance! What did they expect? That the Guardian would remain forever in its primordial slumber?" Now holding her head in her hands, she began breathing deeply, nostrils flaring, in order to rapidly purge away the portent's dizzying energy, not to mention her adrenalin spike.

"Have you recovered sister?" the first asked with concern. A hand steadied her one shoulder, while the other did likewise—unconsciously forming an equilateral triangle.

She nodded, "Ladies, that was *some* double-shot latte."

Ignoring the third's failed attempt at dry humor, the second inquired, "What did you see?"

"Sand. A barren landscape surrounded by steep rocky cliffs. A pitiful truck and two men—father and son. They were trying to pry something away from the Gate. It was then the Guardian took them," she recounted with a shiver, "Savagely."

"Anything else?" the second pushed.

"No. The Gate is safe, intact," said the third.

The first, who had gotten up, returned with three glasses of water. "Here sister. Drink."

"Thank you," said the third with sincerity.

"I have a thought," said the second. "If Portia here received this portent, I wonder who else might have?"

"Surely TIIIS, one of its allies, or a non-aligned for sure," said the first.

"We should think on this," said the second."

"Indeed, Julianna," said Marcia.

*   *   *

Half a world away another had indeed received the portent.

"My word! What idiots!" the wide-eyed far-seer exclaimed with a mixture of shock and appalling dread. "What fool would think to tamper with the Gate to the

Netherworld? The Guardian was full in its rights to destroy them both!" The last declaration was delivered with such outrage that spittle and saliva flew across the water-filled silver basin of the round wooden imaging table. Fortunately, none reached the listener opposite.

Still gripping the table's rounded sides with white knuckles, the fuzzy haired, red-headed far-seer continued. "Mark my words carefully, First Nation Leader, those within the Netherworld took notice. I can see they sense an opportunity not unlike the times of the Great Rent of 1431, when the dark souls first took their illicit release. Dispatch your Lictor of Magic forthwith to defend the Moral Realm from that which is utterly unthinkable."

With a heavy sigh, the far-seer, exhausted by her portent, sagged across the table and commenced to snore like a rough-idling Panzer tank. Within the sensitive's cave, the reverberating racket soon became unbearable to the listener. The petit Navajo First Nation Leader, Betsy Silver Moon remained, too stunned to move. *There is a physical portal to the Netherworld? That's news to me. I'm going to have to visit Mr. Dexter at the Old Oaks campus about this one. Perhaps he can enlighten me.*

The far-seer's cave was located in close proximity to the region's powerful ley line, the Silver Nile, which Silver Moon figured the adept had tapped into. The New Mexican city of Santa Fe was only some twenty minutes away via Interstate 25, her organization's private jet perhaps another ten. While she drove like the wind in that direction, she called ahead from her bright red Colorado to alert the pilots they were soon going to western Pennsylvania and the Arnold Palmer Regional Airport near Latrobe. From there, a quick twenty-minute drive in a southwestern direction and Silver Moon would arrive at the Old Oaks Academy, the intellectual heart and soul of her society. Once there, she would confront Mr. Dexter about what she had just heard.

\*   \*   \*

"Hmm," the tall and gaunt Frenchman hummed at his president's request for information. "I think I have something that might illuminate the question over on that shelf above." He pointed with a long and boney finger, heavily scarred by the searing fire caused by that Hellfire missile attack upon the Academy's chapel. Such was the price Mr. Dexter willingly paid in the defense of several students.

He slowly pushed the ladder on its iron wheels along a shiny track. Its progress easily noted by the office's creaking wooden floor. He stopped at the book's approximate location and began to ascend, and ascend, and ascend some more, on the narrow scaffolding. When one has a two-storey office with shelving that intrudes to the roof beams, this is precisely what you have to occasionally do—climb. Now with his feet fully twenty feet above the office floor, Silver Moon distinctly heard her neck crack as she watched the scarecrow-like man precariously reach over and pluck out a slim volume.

With prize in hand, Mr. Dexter pursed his lips and blew a quick puff that created a minor dust cloud from its upper surface. "Ah, yes. *Monsieur* Aubrey Rubin Le Fey, *Une vue des abysses*, Paris, 1789." Dexter lyrically intoned as if crooning over a rare bottle of red wine. "A truly memorable vintage."

The scholar of lethal defensive and offensive magic sat down again behind his ornate Louis XIV desk on a matching throne-like chair. Ever so carefully he cracked open the brittle little book, while his gaunt face whispered into its frail, yellowed, and aged-spotted pages, which then relaxed open as if bound only the day before.

"President Silver Moon, I must warn you, *Monsieur* Le Fey was not one of us. He was a renegade dark practitioner of the worse sort. Human sacrifice was perhaps his least offense against civilized society. But I do remember a passage that he once wrote that is germane. Allow me just a moment to find it, ah, yes! Here it is. I will translate it to you as it is written in old French." Dexter noisily cleared his throat and began.

It has been told to me by a wretch, that the Dark Environs can be compared to an alchemist's brewing bottle: deep and commodious, full bodied, but with a long and narrow throat at one end.

Finished, the wizard looked up and contentedly smiled, obviously quite pleased with himself.

"Is that all, Henri, surely..." the disbelieving president said.

"*Madam* President," he interrupted, "it is the only remark that I know of regarding the physical nature of the Netherworld."

"It sounds like the 'wretch' you mentioned was drunk as a skunk, while he described an empty wine bottle."

"Indeed, one might be tempted to think so. However, this particular and brief description was pieced together over a rather lengthy period of time.

You see, the 'wretch' that he mentions was the current object of *Monsieur* Le Fey's hobby—torture—and as a consequence, I sincerely believe it."

The president of TIIIS gasped in horror at this tidbit.

"And if I may anticipate your possible objections regarding the veracity of such garnered information, *Monsieur* Le Fey was the personal examiner to the Sun King.

"And there is one other item to consider, *Madam* President. It is my belief *Monsieur* Le Fey lived a long time, was undoubtedly quite old, as in ancient. We know this, because his book was written in the Greek Socratic tradition as a series of conversations. While his literary style might have been an affectation, I sincerely doubt it. For in those conversations, *Monsieur* Le Fey is often referred to as 'Elder Le Fey,' an honorific title that among the Hidden Folk is not granted lightly—hence my surmise of his great age.

"But there is even more. *Monsieur* Le Fey's book would not have seen the light of day unless its author's knowledge was held in high esteem. As happens so often, the perceived quality of a book's contents oftentimes is directly related to its preservation. As a consequence, *Madam* President, I do believe *Monsieur*

Le Fey was a prominent member of the Hidden Folk."

"Really?"

"Indeed madam. It would explain a lot."

"Such as?"

"Such as why the Vatican pursued him so vigorously, eventually capturing the man, 'examining him intensely. They even perversely employed the man's own much beloved hobby, and once they had wrung out of him the very last dram of information, burned him at the stake in the Year of Our Lord 1801."

"Good Lord, how did they justify that?"

"The Vatican does not like Hidden Folk."

"And what of the Guardian of the Dark Realm? What do we know about that?" Silver Moon wondered

Mr. Dexter leaned back deeply into his cushioned chair in thought, tapping his front teeth with a manicured fingernail, as he perused his vast memory.

Finally, "Not much, I fear. But I am quite sure the late Mr. Good would have had some ideas." Then with a brightening of the Frenchman's eyes, "Why not ask Mr. Stone? With his mastery of cuneiform magical texts, he might have brushed up against some reference."

As Silver Moon remained sitting in her chair, the master of offensive and defensive magic realized that there was much more on his president's mind.

"What is so troubling you, my friend?"

A knowing smile, "Even with my mind blocked, you can read me like a newspaper."

A shrug was his only reply.

"I have a very big favor to ask."

*   *   *

While Mr. Dexter's spacious office was located in one corner of Old Main's third floor, Mr. Stone's was on the second of Meyer's, a foreboding Romanesque structure right out of the European Dark Ages. Thickly built, with massive stone walls and arrow-slit windows, just ascending to the second floor required a steep climb up a tightly twisting, and therefore easily defensible, stone staircase.

Within the former office of Mr. Good, an expert of ancient magical texts, Silver Moon found J.J. Stone, Good's former student and now successor. As she stood before his open door, a massively built wooden barrier complete with a caged iron grill, the president took in the virtual monk's cell and its cramped walls covered with shelved books.

"Good afternoon, Mr. Stone." Silver Moon said softly to the top of a deeply-engrossed head of blond hair.

Swiftly looking up, a broad smile bathed the Navajo in emotional warmth that caused the president to blush.

"Betsy! What a surprise!" Stone said with dancing blue eyes. "Come on in and get out of the cold," the near-giant gestured as he stood and cleared a stack of books from the narrow office's sole visitor's chair.

"What's up?" he expectantly asked.

"Serious business, I'm afraid."

Instantly the boyish look disappeared, replaced by the starkly chiseled features of a seasoned warrior. "How bad is it?"

"I have just learned that the Netherworld has a physical gate that opens to our realm of existence."

"Is that even possible?" Stone whispered.

The president confirmed, "Apparently so. And, it has a Guardian as well. Have you encountered anywhere in your studies any mention of such a Guardian of the Netherworld? Mr. Dexter was hopeful you had."

Stone rubbed his chin in thought, then after several moments a look of conviction covered his face. "Yes,

yes, I have, and you'll not like it one bit. In Sumerian, the Guardian of the Netherworld was called this," as he refused to say its name aloud. Instead, he wrote it down on a slip of paper and turned it in Silver Moon's direction.

## KUR

"Betsy this primordial entity had a long snake-like head and sometimes was described as a winged dragon. We know of it from at least three textual traditions. This," pointing to the letters before him, "is serious stuff."

Silver Moon looked down, committed the name to memory, and looked up saying. "I know you have already faced down a dragon over New York City. Is this the same? Or something else altogether?"

"Betsy, I frankly don't know."

"Do you think you're up to taking on this Sumerian dragon-snake thing, Lictor of Magic? I know you have slain an Assyrian griffin demon once."

"Looks like I have no choice, does it, Madam President."

"My thoughts exactly. But before you deploy, be sure to tune up. Don't go walking into this too cocky."

"Ma'am, I read you loud and clear."

*   *   *

President Silver Moon, portent in hand, next approached the Vatican with the news. She *had* to. Only a year before, the Holy Father had extended TIIIS an informal treaty, granting a diplomatic relationship of *bonae voluntatis*, or "good will," because of their society's heroic actions in New York City. Cardinal Jardin, a man who she had never before contacted, held the position of second secretariat within the Holy See. That made him her counterpart, as he directed the operational side of the Brotherhood of St. Paul and Pro Deo—the Vatican's first lines of defense regarding all things paranormal. On the Pro Deo side, a certain Cardinal Alberti reported directly to him.

Silver Moon, uncharacteristically nervous, made the call to Jardin's private line.

*"Ciao. Questo è Jardin."*

"Cardinal Jardin. This is President Betsy Silver Moon of TIIIS. Your Eminence, do you speak English?"

After a brief pause and a few quick key strokes on his computer, "Why yes, I do. What can I do for you *Signora Presidente* Silver Moon?" With those key strokes Jardin had pulled up a picture of the caller on his laptop's screen. It was an old habit from his days in

Vatican counter-intelligence. The man liked to know what a caller looked like. He felt it gave him an edge. The face before him carried an earnest and honest look.

"Your Eminence, my society was recently granted a special relationship with the Holy See by the Holy Father."

"Ah yes, *Signora Presidente*, of this I am aware."

Now hearing the cardinal's speech pattern Silver Moon made a point of being as clear as possible, as from the sound of it, English may have been the cleric's fifth language after Latin, Italian, French, and German.

"As an act of good will, my society wishes to inform yours of some recent information I think you will find of interest."

"Yes."

"We have learned of a potential threat to the Dark and Mortal Realms. Someone attempted to open a physical, and not *metaphysical*, breach between the realms."

"*What?*"

"Additionally, Your Eminence, this attempted breach occurred somewhere in the Western Desert of Egypt."

"*Where?*"

"Your Eminence, while we do not know the precise location of this attempted breach, we intend to deploy assets to the region to find and hopefully stop the unthinkable from occurring."

There was a prolonged pause from the cardinal's end of the line. Silver Moon swore that she could hear furious typing in the background.

"I see, *Signora Presidente*. I have just checked. We have no information regarding this matter at this time. I can assure you that the Vatican is in your debt. Please tell me more."

"Earlier today, one of our far-seers informed me of the situation. She was extremely agitated about it. Apparently, some grave robbers desecrated a desert monument in some way. The Guardian of the Netherworld reacted. They disappeared as a result. We can only conclude that they are dead."

*"Deo meo ... "* the cleric groaned into the receiver. "Does your society wish assistance in this matter?"

"Yes, Your Eminence, very much so. If you could lend us someone with an Egyptological background that would be most helpful."

"I see. When do you intend to deploy?"

"In one week."

Silver Moon now distinctly heard the cardinal typing over the line.

"I see. *Signora Presidente*, you are in luck. We indeed have such a resource on staff. In two days expect a communication from Cardinal Alberti. His name is: A-L-B-E-R-T-I. He will be your contact henceforth regarding this matter. Good day, *Signora Presidente*."

After Jardin hung up, his fingers flew as he composed a terse e-mail to his subordinate, Albert.

> Guille:
>
> Within the week, prepare Dr. Reissen for deployment.
>
> Munitions training authorized.
>
> Specifics to follow.

\*   \*   \*

Deep within the Dark Realm, the Devourer of Souls stirred with interest. Master of that domain by divine design, it remained never sated. The dark primordial nurtured dark souls and engendered demons of all kinds in anticipation of their summoning by unwitting mortals. It and they yearned for the day when they would again escape beyond the primordial boundaries established by the Creator. Nonetheless, its subjects cheered in unison at the Guardian's recent agitation, hoping for another breach, this time physical. But several safeguards remained that blocked their safe passage.

The first was the all too tangible presence and ferocity of the Guardian itself, an entity formed by the Creator for the purpose. This stalwart entity cared not for the Netherworld's inhabitants and somehow, even less for its master. No words or promises could turn this incorruptible one aside to let them pass.

Another was the Ledger Keeper, the counter of souls, who tabulated the comings and goings of all spiritual and demonic emanations between the Dark, Light, and Moral Realms. By divine design its ledger must balance. Otherwise, it would invite imbalance between the realms and the threat of a rent forming between them—an awful prospect, but one that had once occurred, but had been remedied and repaired.

Finally, the enforcer of the balance between the realms was none other than the First Soul of Creation, an entity specifically created for the purpose—a fearless demon-slayer. Most irksome, the First Soul currently resided within the Lictor of Magic, the individual who had recently sealed the rent between the Dark and Mortal Realms. This mortal had claimed many demons with his sword, wrecked carnage among dark practitioners, and the Devourer of Souls too, wanted his due.

# CHAPTER 9

Five and a half months into my psychic immersion at the Vatican, I received a forwarded email from Inspector Ali Hassan of the Egyptian Archaeological Service. Marta, my Viennese departmental secretary, had thoughtfully passed it on.

Greetings from Sakkara Dr. Reissen!

I and my staff truly miss you. Not that your colleague Dr. Gretchen Gunner is not doing an excellent job with the investigations at the Temple of Ptah. It's just you are so approachable, imaginative, and insightful.

Reissen thought, *Now that's an odd remark. I'm going to have to talk to Gretch. Get her to lighten up a bit. Get her to bury some of that Teutonic enthusiasm of hers.*

Allow me to be direct, Dr. Reissen. One week ago a chance discovery was made in the Western Desert. Being as it fell to my jurisdiction, and that my staff is stretched like a taut bow string, I immediately thought about how you and your team had come to the aid of my predecessor, Inspector Kama, with the Djedi tomb.

Dr. Reissen, would you consider returning to Egypt, visiting the site, and perhaps, taking on this opportunity? Be assured that I will do everything in my power to make your visit comfortable and worthwhile.

Sincerely yours,

Ali Hassan
Inspector, Sakkaran Archaeological District


To say I was torn by Hassan's offer would be an understatement. After all, how many foreign Egyptologists are invited to take on an investigation straight out-of-the-blue? Answer: in this day and age— not many. In fact, right off the top of my head, I could not think of any. The professional downstream ramifications boggled my mind.

If I took on the project, what would it lead to, and for how long? Where would the funding come from? How would I staff it? Gretchen has all my veterans from the Djedi tomb, who now are hard at work in Memphis. On the other hand, if I did not take on the project, how would that affect my long-term relationship with my good friend Ali, who clearly was in a bind? And for that matter, how would such a refusal reverberate within the highly political cauldron that is the Egyptian Archaeological Service?

My hesitation was fueled by my current situation. I could feel myself transforming under the tutelage of the Pro Deo staff. At the same time I found myself at the cusp of grasping my hidden paranormal self. In short, I was damned if I did, and damned if I didn't. So I went on a long walk through the City to clear my head, all the while hoping for some enlightenment.

For those unfamiliar with Vatican City, it is a self-contained universe of its own: narrow cobblestone streets; centuries-old buildings with more than the patina of age, but of history as well; its own post; occasional copse of tall and fragrant pine; pigeons abound begging for popcorn or bread—they're not fussy; its own army; tight groups of clergy and laity walk with purpose and converse, heads together, in hushed tones; flowering gardens, some hidden, others not; and throughout the amazing aura of heady tradition and religiosity that binds everything together.

After a bit, I just sat down on the stone bench beneath the obelisk in Saint Peter's Square. It seemed appropriate, as the monument has no hieroglyphs engraved on it, as a consequence has no known owner, and is only suspected to be originally from Heliopolis. In short, the nameless obelisk was as clueless as me. As I stared up its regular and smoothed flanks, I felt a kinship with its anonymity. It was a blank slate, like me. But unlike myself, I still could engrave a new set of glyphs unto my psyche. Besides, I was so close to a psychic breakthrough that I could taste it. So then and there, beneath the nameless obelisk, I decided to turn down Ali's offer.

*   *   *

Two weeks later my probationary six-month sojourn within the Vatican's walls ended. Cardinal Alberti, prompt as a clock, summoned me to his office. Like an errant school boy being told to report to the principal, I entered the cleric's suite uncertain and with a lump in my throat. I had worked hard and consequently knew all too well that I had a lot to lose.

"*Signora*," I managed to croak out to his secretary, "I have been informed His Eminence wishes to speak to me."

"Your name please?"

"Reissen. Erik Reissen."

After consulting her computer, she smiled, *"Uno momento Herr Dr.* Reissen," as she sent a message.

As I awkwardly stood before her desk with my hands behind my back, only now did I notice the rich Persian rug beneath my feet, the exquisite woodwork around the doors and baseboards, the polish of the brass doorknob and its plate, and their worn patina. Turning to the open window, a tall pine scented the room. A bird's nest, filled with screeching open-mouthed young, perched precariously on one branch. *Just like me.*

*"Herr* Reissen?" the secretary snapped me out of my reverie.

*"Ja?"*

"His Eminence will see you now."

Approaching the door, I respectfully knocked twice, waited a beat until I heard, *"Entrare,"* and only then did so. I also had rested my palm against his door for that split second. His Eminence, I could clearly tell, was keyed up—something good to know.

Since beginning with my training, I had relearned so many things, like how to read body language and blend it with my sixth sense to build a 3D image of an individual. First impressions, while vital, are just that. Second meetings tended to be more concrete, as more back story was available. Within these walls the cardinal's psychic abilities had become legend, making him a perfect operations manager for Pro Deo.

\* \* \*

*This Reissen is entirely a different breed,* Alberti thought with a mix of pleasure and uncertainty as he reviewed the Austrian's thick dossier and its glowing recommendations from his instructors.

*Definite hybrid material. Sister Gabriella was spot on.*

Nonetheless, first impressions remained important, for the cleric remembered quite vividly the first time he had set eyes on the man. Tall, fit, tanned, and physically dominating, yet emanating such a raw psychic vibration.

*His mere handshake was positively electric!*

His laptop chimed a message from his secretary. "Dr. Reissen is here—five minutes early."

The cardinal unconsciously grunted at the news and scratched the side of his nose. *So Austrian, but once we are through, he might want those five minutes back. So much is about to happen.*

He typed his reply, waited a moment, and sent it back to his secretary.

*This will be interesting.* He thought as he

rearranged his desk and folded his hands before him.

He heard a probing double knock. *Let the games begin.*

*"Entrare."*

The cleric's second impression was as if a ghost had entered his office. There was Reissen, clearly, but the man was totally under control, guarded, and wary. He had suppressed his energetic psychic bubble and blocked his thoughts ... *What a transformation ... and so quickly,* he amended as he blocked his own as well.

"Please take a seat, Dr. Reissen." The cleric gestured, "We have much to discuss."

"Dr. Reissen, this thick file to my right is yours." The cardinal indicated with a tip of his head. "We now know who you are, what you are, and what you might become."

Sliding the file over in front of him, Alberti opened it with a theatrical flip of his forefinger. "Since your arrival at Pro Deo, you have done well. All of your instructors have rated you as ... 'Satisfactory.'" That statement was a bald lie, for in actual fact the documents before him clearly stated two "Excellent" and one "Most Satisfactory" ratings.

"Thank you, Your Eminence. I had the benefit of many fine instructors, especially Sister Gabriella. She really knew how to bust my balls," Reissen drily stated.

*I just bet she did.*

Alberti sensed a flicker of emotion with Reissen's remark and truly appreciated the comment, since that diminutive nun had nearly broken his as well.

"Yes, well," Alberti began while leaning forward against the worn brown leather of his desk pad. "I have summoned you to inform you that you have successfully passed your probationary term and now are officially a member of Pro Deo. While you still have much to learn, we have discovered that the best teacher is experience gained in the field. As a consequence, I wish to inform you of your first deployment. To be blunt, Dr. Reissen, your beloved Egypt needs you. In one week's time, you will be there as part of an international team headed by your colleague Sister Josephina Busby."

Reissen's surprise at the news did not show. The Austrian remained a mute cipher. *Such control,* so Alberti continued.

"Prior to your departure, you will be reintroduced to firearms by the armorer of the Swiss Guard. Train well and quickly. You just never know in this day and age." The cleric concluded with a raised eyebrow for emphasis.

After a lengthy pause, Reissen asked. "What is the nature of the threat, Your Eminence?"

*Ah, he has not lost that Austrian directness.*

"A potential psychic event is brewing in the Egyptian Western Desert. Someone attempted to violate the Gate of the Netherworld. They paid for that indiscretion with their lives. Among other things, it will be your job to assess the situation and calm things down."

Reissen frowned, "Your Eminence, I have felt nothing of the sort."

"True enough, Dr. Reissen. What I am describing is a potential future breach. Our team's job is to prevent such a catastrophic event from happening."

# CHAPTER 10

She decided to call it Project Damokles. It seemed fitting—a threat from above and all that. The selection of volunteers for the undertaking was not an easy one for Betsy Silver Moon, for it meant certain death for most of them, if not all. Even if someone somehow managed to survive the initial onslaught, it was judged doubtful that an individual would survive long term given the extraordinary strain of the experience. The qualities of youthful strength and endurance mixed with hard-earned experience do not often coincide. Yet, that critical combination was precisely what the Navajo looked for.

At the final cut, the TIIIS president had not thirty, but forty-six volunteers. They came from TIIIS' ranks, non-aligned paranormal entities, and to her ultimate surprise, Chairman William DeSalvo of CMES. In an obvious show of paranormal solidarity, he offered six of his organization's best.

Based upon the Pentagon's shared telemetry, her plan needed at least thirty individuals with the appropriate qualifications to undertake the task at hand. Each pairing would work in isolation, geographically sprinkled along the asteroid's predicted shadow, while linked directly to a ley line—to boost their psychic potential. These "telekinetic channelers," would work in concert, in layered pairings, all additionally guided by remote-viewers who aided them in their efforts to affect the path of the speeding asteroid. That was the plan. Their purpose: every meter of achieved deflection would grant the Earth's billions a greater chance for survival.

*   *   *

Fully sixteen months before the arrival of the asteroid called Gravitron, Silver Moon had had an earnest conversation with one of her most trusted colleagues.

"Mr. Dexter, how would you propose the twenty-three pairings prepare for the asteroid's arrival?"

Through steepled fingers the master of offensive and defensive magic slowly answered. "Slowly, carefully and with a gradually building intensity. Remember, Madam President, these pairings must learn to instinctively work as one. Yes, we have over one year to prepare, but I would counsel that we begin tomorrow in their psychic binding. By that, I mean each pairing must learn how to focus upon a fast approaching object. That takes practice. Each pairing must learn to concentrate their telekinetic force together, in unison, and without qualm. In other words, more practice on real and ever more difficult targets. Finally, each pairing must work directly with their ley line, establishing its trust over time. Each pairing must form an understanding with their semi-sentient ley line that when the time comes, it will channel, come what may, as much power as the pairing can withstand, and then, perhaps even more. Such tangible psychic exertion will claim many. The self-aware ley lines are not accustomed to burning out those with whom it has an abiding relationship. This they must come to understand as well. All of this will take time, a commodity that is fast disappearing."

The Frenchman then paused to gather his thoughts.

"When you think about it, Madam President, there is much to do. And we have yet to devise a technical communication system that will reliably join the pairings, so that their best efforts can be coordinated. That will also take some doing—and practice."

"Will you take on this effort, Mr. Dexter? Train our pairings? And coordinate their exertions?" Silver Moon quietly asked.

Head bowed, the old Frenchman softly replied, *Oui, Madam* President. It would be my honor to do so. But I will need resources and assistance. Despite what you might think, I still can only be in one place at a time."

"Thank you, Henri. Begin the training immediately. Let me know whatever you require."

# CHAPTER 11

While TIIIS busied themselves with the recruitment, screening, and selection of their telekinetic channeling teams, the Joint Chiefs were also hard at work. But they soon found their biggest problem was one of sheer scale, as the rest of the world wanted in on the defense of the planet.

Proposals ran the gamut from ballistic missiles with nuclear payloads, to orbital laser platforms, to the extraterrestrial attachment of solar sails. Each had their adherents, each their detractors. No one dared to mention that all of these schemes were purely theoretical and that none of them had been practically tested.

Almost immediately, came the jockeying for resources. At stake was whose political district or state would build or deliver which component, much less who would take ultimate command. The waters all quickly muddied to the point that fourteen months out, no one really knew if *anything* was on the drawing board, much less in the works. The media pundits had a field day with this Gordian Knot, sniping here and there at will. One even remarked, "And so ends the human race, caused by self-serving bureaucratic paralysis by analysis."

*　　*　　*

One billionaire, however, positively fumed at the pathetic situation. She had an idea, an in-house team, the independent resources, and the audacious will to execute it. Already heavily invested in modern aviation and reusable rocket development, the thrust of her idea was to blatantly borrow from Hollywood, perform a flyby of Gravitron while it was still in deep space, affix a nuclear device to the object, and detonate it. Clearly understood from the start as a suicide mission, Jane Jarvis, a freakishly bright physicist and a woman who did not reward failure, already held in her hand the personnel records of over twenty highly-qualified volunteers. All wanted the chance to fly the mission.

Sixteen months out, Jarvis brainstormed with her staff over a long weekend. On the following Monday she ran the numbers, and after some consideration, went with it. The project was just Jarvis' cup of tea—high risk with the potential for an astronomically high reward. After a quiet meeting with the President of the

United States, she was given a one hundred kiloton device, its delivery system, and the silent blessing of the American people. Her projected launch date—ten months prior to what had become known worldwide as Zero Hour.

After a feverish development sprint unlike anything known in modern history, Jarvis Industries secretly and successfully launched its rocket, payload, and command crew from Vandenberg Air Force Base fully eleven months prior to Zero Hour. Lavish bonuses were quietly disbursed to the members of the project team—all the way down to the three cleared janitors.

In attendance in the launch command bunker were the President of the United States, his Joint Chiefs, Jarvis, and her senior staff. As the rocket's pillar of flame ascended into the heavens, so did their hopes and prayers for its success.

# CHAPTER 12

"So where the hell am I supposed to go?" the impatient Lictor of Magic wanted to know.

"Mr. Stone, all I have been told is that a Vatican representative will meet you in the public concourse once you get through customs." One of his pilots said over his shoulder. His partner was still attempting to fill out a clip board full of landing and provisioning paperwork.

Stone had just landed with the TIIIS private jet at the private side of the Cairo International Airport. As for the Lictor of Magic, he was raring to go, to get in the field, and save the world once again. The eleven-hour flight had been difficult on him. He dearly missed his daily five mile run. Fortunately, his urban combat suit (UCS), its associated weaponry, and sword had been sent ahead via diplomatic channels. The Abdel Fattah al-Sissy regime had cracked down on the importation of any such items that might be misconstrued as terrorist arms.

This end of the airport had its own passport control. Standing at six two, the strapping blond-headed man had nowhere to hide as the Egyptian security police eyed him with suspicion.

Presenting his US passport at the kiosk, the mustached Egyptian official asked, "What is the nature of your visit, Mr … Stone?"

"Tourism."

"Your hotel?"

"Nile Hilton," Stone invented.

"Enjoy your stay in Egypt. Next." The official said with a wave, his focus on Stone already passed.

The American retrieved his wheelie and breezed by several Egyptian soldiers at port-arms and full body armor as he left baggage. *This is one tense environment. Those dudes are alert.* He entered the public concourse through double-sliding glass doors. Amid the line of well-wishers, it didn't take long for the Vatican representative to find him.

"Mr. Stone? Is that you, Mr. Stone?" a short nun in a black and white habit asked.

"I'm Stone, sister. Who are you?"

"Sister Josephina Busby," she said, showing him a laminated ID card. "I'm with the Vatican. I'm your contact and team lead. May I see your passport?"

Stone blinked perhaps a bit too obviously.

"You have a problem with that mister?" Busby snapped while looking up at him. "You've seen mine. So show me yours?"

Struggling not to laugh, "No ma'am, I mean, Sister Busby," he retrieved the document from his back pocket.

"Thank you Mr. Stone. We're all good. By the way, never carry your passport in a back pocket. It's too easily picked. Now, I understand the rest of your gear is waiting for you over at diplomatic stores. I'll take you there."

\*   \*   \*

Nun or not, Stone was impressed with Busby's driving from the airport to the western suburbs of Cairo. Three times en route he had either stomped a phantom brake pedal on the Toyota Land Cruiser's floorboards, or winced in preparation for impact. Neither occurred as the Vatican representative possessed terrific reflexes and an uncanny ability to anticipate gaps in traffic.

Finally, Stone piped up. "Sister Busby."

"Yeah."

"You're one damn good driver. Ever consider a career in NASCAR?"

"Thanks, but no. Those dudes drive too slow for me. So tell me about that sword of yours."

"It has a core of Damascus steel with a bonded ceramic blade impregnated with silver."

"That makes you a demon-slayer."

"Yep, that's me."

"What else do you have up your sleeve?"

"I'm a kinetic telepath trained in lethal magic … and I can translocate."

"Through solid objects!"

"No, just through space."

"Oh. Is there anything else that I should know about you?"

"I'm a published authority on Sumerian and Akkadian magical texts."

*"Really?"*

"Yeah. Have you ever heard of the book, *Curses and Demons: Dark Magic from Ancient Mesopotamia*?"

"You bet!" the nun said with familiarity. "That text is required reading among the paranormal community. That book is *yours*?"

"Yep."

"My God. I'm chauffeuring around a *New York Times* best-selling author. Mr. Stone, you're really quite a package."

"Thanks."

"I can't wait to introduce you to the rest of the team. By the way, that platinum aura of yours is awesome."

*   *   *

As Busby pulled up into the circular drive of the Mena House Gardens Hotel, Stone was taken by the hotel's green manicured grounds, the near-suffocating scent of sweet blooming flowers, and the imposing presence of the Giza Pyramids. Since it was dusky dark, they were backlit by the last rays of the setting sun. The effect took his breath away.

Craning his neck around like an owl, Stone couldn't help himself, "Are those the real thing?"

"Yep," Busby chirped in imitation.

"Pictures don't do 'em justice."

"You got that right mister."

Pulling to a stop, Busby got out, accepted a valet chit, and dropped her keys into the manicured hand of a starched white-coated attendant, while Stone gathered up his gear from the back.

"Follow me, Mr. Stone. Are you hungry?" She said over her shoulder.

"Starved."

"Good. The rest of the team is waiting for us on the terrace."

*   *   *

The terrace restaurant at the Mena House provided another view of its well-groomed grounds, fragrant flower beds, cabanas, and its amoeba-shaped swimming pool. As ludicrous as it may seem, I saw over a neighboring wall a nine-hole golf course near the base of the Great Pyramid.

As we approached I counted five people sitting around a long white linen table sipping a variety of drinks under a darkening blue and cloudless sky. The sun had set, painting the heavens with streamers of orange backed by a sky full of stars.

Out of habit, I scanned everyone at the table. Among them were two powerful sensitives. Busby's aura glowed like a nuclear furnace. Instinctively, I first approached the fit middle-aged guy with black hair, stuck out my hand and said, "I'm Stone."

Rising from his chair, the man, who had a bright teal aura, took it firmly, and said with a heavy accent and a nod, "Reissen. Erik Reissen. Pleasure to meet you. Please, sit," as he gestured to the open chair next to him at the table's end. Before I did, I rested my gear in it in preparation of making the rounds, but Sister Busby beat me to it.

"Everyone, please welcome Mr. J.J. Stone to our team. He has a unique set of skills," she said eyeing me, "but his biggest is that he's an expert in Sumerian and Akkadian magical spells, *and*, a best-selling *New York Times* author."

That last brought forth some wide eyes and some suspicious ones as well. I quickly figured out Sister Busby wanted to take charge of the meal, meeting, whatever, and perhaps make me squirm a bit. With her mind blocked, I couldn't tell. So I just smiled, waved to everyone, rearranged my gear behind my chair, and sat down by the guy named 'Reissen, Erik Reissen.'

"Now everyone, please introduce yourselves." Busby orchestrated.

*Yep. I was right.*

To my immediate right sat a willowy and attractive red-head with a lime green aura that screamed creativity and art.

"Hello, Mr. Stone," she said with an accent I couldn't place while offering her hand, "My name is Else Wald. I'm the team's photographer and videographer." Since the woman had pronounced her last name with a distinctive V-sound, that marked her as either German, Austrian, or something similar. Maybe even South African.

"Pleasure to meet you, ma'am."

Looking to the person next to Wald, she piped up. "Hi, I'm Sheila Roth." *An American accent.* "I'm a colleague of Sister Josephina." *No kidding, I thought. Definitely a strong sensitive with that blazing red aura!* "Egyptian religion and magic are my specialties."

"Again, it's a pleasure."

The lanky blond man next to Roth rose, reached over his hand, and formally said, "Welcome. I am Franks, Willi Franks." *Definite German accent. Those V's again.* "I am a surveyor." *And your disturbed aura also says you don't like me sitting next to Wald. Log that.*

At the opposite end of the table sat Sister Busby, so I just nodded in her direction. To her right, sat a short brown-haired man who also offered his hand. "Hallo, Mr. Stone, I am Jürgen Peters, the other surveyor," he managed to say with a broad grin. *Definitely another German with a blue aura that said "pure science." My money says he's Franks' team lead.*

Next to Peters sat a man with a bushy mustache that I judged to be in his mid-thirties. Without question he was an Egyptian with a warm light blue aura. "Mr.

Stone," he stood and extended his hand, "I am Inspector Ali Hassan of the Sakkaran Archaeological District. Welcome to Egypt and our table." *What a flat out nice guy.*

Finally, the man to my left reintroduced himself and the way the rest of the table unconsciously deferred to him, including Sister Busby, spoke volumes. "Mr. Stone, I am Dr. Erik Reissen. I am an archaeologist and Egyptologist. And I too am very interested in Egyptian magic. Welcome to our team." With another firm handshake, this time chock-full of psychic energy, I didn't need to reread his teal-colored aura. He was the clear natural leader of this pack.

The introductions were followed by an awkward silence that was finally broken by the befreckled red-head Wald.

"So, Mr. Stone, what does J.J. stand for?"

*Perfect question! So I laid it on thick in the slow and thick drawl of Texas.*

"Well, Ms. Wald, thank you for asking. J.J. stands for Jonathan Joseph. And since that's quite a mouthful to say all the time, all my friends in Texas just called me J.J. And from where I'm sitting, you-all look mighty friendly. So from now on, I'm just J.J."

That broke the ice. Even Franks seemed to relax some.

*   *   *

"So, why are we all here?" Sister Busby rhetorically asked. "Inspector Hassan, would you kindly fill us in?"

"Yes," while nodding in her direction, "Thank you, Sister Busby. I shall. Approximately two weeks ago, two men, a father and son, tragically went missing. Within the week, their abandoned pickup truck was found next to an unknown structure in the Western Desert. As the Inspector of Sakkara, that structure is my responsibility. So I contacted my good friend here, Dr. Reissen, to investigate it and he has agreed. And now here we are. Tomorrow we begin. Dr. Reissen?"

"Thank you, Inspector Hassan. And it is good to be back in Egypt. Tomorrow we will meet here for breakfast at five." This was met with several groans, which the Austrian ignored. "Thereafter, given that there will be seven of us, and with all of our luggage and equipment, we will take two vehicles to the site. To say that I am excited about this opportunity to again assist the Egyptian Archaeological Service," nodding to Hassan, "would be an understatement. My suggestion to all is to get sufficient sleep, because I can guarantee tomorrow will be a busy day. Are there any questions?"

"Where is the site?" Franks wanted to know.

"About a kilometer and a half west of the Stepped Pyramid of Sakkara," Inspector Hassan shared. "The vehicles we will be using are borrowed from the Egyptian military, as they are the most rugged for such a journey. We will be traveling overland, through the desert. Please do not forget to sufficiently hydrate before leaving the hotel."

"Any other questions? Reissen probed.

"Are we staying here for the rest of the project?" Roth hoped.

"No." the archaeologist answered, "Pack up all of your luggage and gear for the journey south. Our next hotel will be in the Memphis area, where we will meet up with our colleagues on the Austrian archaeological mission."

# CHAPTER 13

The next morning the expedition mounted up on two Hummers painted in tan desert camouflage. Franks, Peters, Wald, and Roth went in one, the rest in the other. Both vehicles had tactical radios. Inspector Hassan, however, would meet the convoy at the entrance into the desert and join them there.

The Alpha-Hummer was operated by Franks who had done considerable driving while in the German military, while Reissen took on the driving duties of the Beta. Without question, the vehicles were noticed as they wound their way through the creeping traffic along the western side of the Nile River. Both tourists and locals alike gaped at them sitting high and wide on the narrow roads, at times even blocking traffic whenever the big tourist buses tried to get past. Surprisingly, no paint was transferred.

The dominant conversation in the Alpha predictably centered on Stone, the outsider—who he was, what did he bring to the table, and why he was there.

"I think he's an imbedded reporter," Franks said.

"No, that can't be," said Roth waving her hands in negation, "he's a credentialed academic with a big book on ancient magic. So the real question is—why is he here? That's what I what to know. He's not an Egyptologist or an archaeologist."

"I think he's handsome," Wald simply stated with a little smile, which caused Franks' knuckles to turn white on the steering wheel.

"He's certainly big enough, looks fit enough, to handle a shovel. That's all *I* need to know," Peters said dismissively. "I am not an archaeologist nor want to be one. I just survey and make maps."

Meanwhile in the Beta-Hummer, the conversation was far more serious.

"I suspect, Mr. J.J.," the form of address that Reissen settled on, "that there is far more to you than books and magical texts," he challenged with an eye-glance into the rearview mirror.

Stone said nothing as he lounged in the backseat taking in the passing landscape. Sister Josephina, now dressed in a baggy tan shirt and slacks, who sat in the passenger's seat, jumped in with both feet.

"Erik, there's something that you should know. We work for the Vatican, correct?"

A curt head nod from the driver.

"J.J. works for an outfit called TIIIS, a secular paranormal organization, who asked for the Vatican's assistance in investigating this archaeological site."

"Sister Josephina, if that were the case, then why is Mr. J.J. here? This is not his cultural turf, Iraq is." He finished with an open-handed gesture.

"Dr. Reissen … Erik …" Stone interjected, "I am here to lend some muscle, perhaps some comparative cultural insights. But above all, I'm here to protect this expedition from anything unexpected."

"Protect us? From what? *With* what?" Reissen pressed with concern.

"Erik, in my organization, I am referred to as a Lictor of Magic. That title grants me the mandate to defend the innocent from evil. That makes me an enforcer for that which is good."

"And how can *you* discern good from evil?" Reissen quizzed.

"It's not easy, sir. It surely isn't a black and white proposition. It took time, study, practice, experience in-the-field, and a ton of common sense to discern the difference." Stone paused. " Even then, Erik, I still make mistakes. The bottom line is this—I'm good at what I do. The ability to read auras helps a bunch.'

Unconvinced, the headstrong driver just grunted.

"Erik," the nun said, "J.J. is here to help us. Isn't that good enough?"

"*Ja.* It is," the stiff Austrian admitted, "but from what, that is my question."

"Erik," Stone began, "I really don't know myself. I'm as blind as a bat. But hopefully this structure will tell us. Maybe we'll find an inscription. But I do know this. Two men disappeared without a trace a couple of weeks ago at that site. My question for you is this—if I hadn't come, how would have you defended your people?"

"I am armed," Reissen quickly said.

"So am I. Thank you for doubling our defensive firepower."

"Mr. J.J., you do not sound like an academic to me. Who are you really?"

"At forty-four years old, I'm many things. I was an only child born and raised on a horse ranch in north Texas. That makes me a Southern Baptist. Out of high school I joined the US Marines and proudly served my country for twelve years. I was discharged a full sergeant with a Silver Star at the ripe old age of thirty. Then I went to college, studied hard, and became a Sumerologist. My publications center on early cuneiform texts dealing with dark magic. Then I joined TIIIS to fight the paranormal powers of evil. What's *your* story?"

The question stunned Reissen. Never before had someone painted him into a corner so easily and so well. While he found the words, they came out woodenly.

"I too was born as an only child into a loving family in an Austrian mountain village. At eighteen I served two years in the Austrian army. Then I went to university, did well, and got a research fellowship at the Vatican's Pontifical College. That's where I first met Sister Josephina. We were students together and became good friends. I continued with my studies and was hired by my university. I have been there ever since."

"So Erik, why Egyptology? Why archaeology?" Stone asked.

"Stone tools, Mr. J.J. I collected them as a boy in the plowed fields of Austria, but they could not speak to me. Egypt's stone tools did."

Sister Josephina sat mesmerized. Never before had she heard Reissen open up like this, much less to practically a stranger.

"And why Sumerology, Mr. J.J.? Why cuneiform?"

"Oh, that one's easy. During the First Iraq War I jumped into a shell crater to escape enemy fire. There I accidently touched an ancient artifact, a soul container to be exact. Well, that container was full and I was promptly possessed by an ancient Sumerian scribe and astronomer. He had lost his wife during a raid on his town. I helped him find the remains of his wife."

"You were possessed by an *ancient?*" Sister Josephina exclaimed while spinning around in her seat to face him.

"Yeah, sort of, it was more a merging of two souls than anything else. Fortunately, it was a benign relationship, but believe you me it really freaked out the military shrinks!"

"What was it like, Mr. J.J., being possessed .. merged?" Reissen asked in total fascination.

"Like having a second self, who would argue, laugh, berate, and encourage you. Good old Nergal taught me a lot. He was a master scribe and taught me a whole bunch of scribal tricks."

"Are you still merged?" Sister Josephina probed now with a furrowed brow.

"Nope. Once we, that is Nergal and me, found the location of his wife's remains, he jilted me, and reunited with her soul. Together they rose from the

Dark Realm into the Light."

"Mr. J.J., are you referring to the cosmology of *The Knot of Eternity*?" the Austrian asked.

"Yep, that's the book, and trust me Erik, it's the real deal. By the way, one of my thesis advisors was Mr. Theodore Good. He wrote the commentary on *The Knot*."

At this news Reissen clammed up and focused on his driving. This outsider was far more than what he seemed. His confident and easy manner annoyed the Egyptologist, who at the same time marveled at the man's impressive pedigree, all the while unfairly measuring himself against it.

As the driver of the Beta-Hummer fumed, Stone listened in on it. *Why oh why do people beat themselves up so? Reissen is a solid player, but he can't always be the tip of the spear. That is not his role. Not here. He's got a lot to learn.*

Meanwhile, Sister Josephina silently sat back to observe this testosterone-filled tennis match, took notes, and read lips.

\* \* \*

True to his word, a smiling and waving Inspector Hassan greeted their small caravan on the side of a secondary road that skirted along the open desert. With a small backpack over his shoulder, he mounted the Beta-Hummer and settled in next to Stone.

Leaning forward, Hassan spoke to Reissen's right ear. "Erik, move up front and take the lead. We will be driving inland for about a kilometer and a half. I will direct you."

Stone then piped up, "Inspector, shouldn't we have our radios on for communications?"

"Ah, good idea, Mr. Stone. Sister Busby, please select 243.000 Megahertz."

"Mega what?" the nun said. "Where do I ...?"

Reissen reached over, made the selection, and flipped on the radio with practiced precision.

"Sister Josephina. Do you want me to get out and set up the other vehicle's radio?" Stone offered.

"Yes, please do."

While Stone was busy with the other vehicle, Reissen admitted to Sister Busby, "Yes, I believe it is good thing to have a veteran on our team."

Once Stone returned, Reissen pulled away from the road's shoulder, and took the lead.

As they trundled along, Inspector Hassan pointed out a natural saddle in the limestone plateau to their right.

"*Erik*, that's it,' Hassan said excitedly. "Turn off in about twenty meters and head straight for it." This the Austrian did and immediately their once smooth boulevard ride transformed into a swaying, bumpy, slow-motion rollercoaster experience.

Meanwhile, Stone was filled with flashbacks of barreling across the Iraqi desert. Sister Josephina was glad she had an open window next to her. Hassan's head just lolled with the terrain. Reissen, however, was having the time of his life. He ramped up the vehicle's speed, putting it into low gear, and took on the slope leading up to the saddle. Sawing the steering wheel as the Beta-Hummer ascended, Reissen grinned like a little kid. He even caught some air as the five thousand pound-plus beast crested the ridge.

Stone, sensing Reissen's pure joy, let out a loud cowboy yell of "Yahoo!" and followed it up with, "Nice wheel work, Erik! That was awesome!"

The Alpha-Hummer that followed needed two attempts before it crested, much to Willi Franks' embarrassment.

With both Hummers now in the saddle, Hassan pointed the way, and the Egyptologist drove.

The trek forward went slowly in the variable conditions of wind-blown rocky gravels and deep fluffy sand, but Reissen rapidly got the hang of the Hummer's abilities and gradually sped up. Before they knew it, the convoy was kicking up gravel and blasting through sand as if they were water puddles. Glancing into the rearview mirror, the archaeologist saw two things— Franks was keeping up nicely and Mr. J.J. was grinning like a kid on holiday.

After about five minutes of this, Reissen's chest suddenly constricted, causing him to get off the gas and roll the Hummer to a gentle halt. Seeing this, the Alpha-Hummer stopped behind them as well, several yards back.

"What's wrong Erik?" Sister Josephina asked with concern as the man slumped over the wheel.

"Something's very wrong. Not with me, but ahead. Great danger. We have to turn back." Reissen gasped out.

Stone firmly said, "Sister Busby, this is why I'm here. Let me take a look ahead." Now looking the nun directly in the eyes, "Get on the radio sister. Keep everyone in the Hummers. Do not allow anyone to disembark. No, absolutely *forbid* them to do so. Understood?"

The nun returned a quick nod of affirmation.

\* \* \*

Dropping the Beta-Hummer's tailgate, Stone rummaged around, found his long duffle bag, and zipped it open. He removed a long and slender object and an indistinct bundle. Then and there, in full view, Stone stripped down to his shorts, much to the glee of Wald, who sat in the passenger's seat of the Alpha-Hummer. The red-head poorly stifled a moan with a hand over her mouth. Until now, she had no idea how ripped the blond-haired American was. She clearly approved.

Franks, with white knuckles on the wheel, bluntly said to no one in particular, "What the hell is he doing? Sister Busby just told us to stay put no matter what." Meanwhile, Stone climbed into some sort of one-piece garment, but as he did, he slowly disappeared from sight.

"How did he do that?" Peters exclaimed, as only Stone's head remained visible, seemingly disembodied and floating in thin air. Then it disappeared as well as Stone's head gear locked into place.

"And now he's totally gone." Roth unnecessarily interjected. "That dude is just full of surprises. Best-selling author my ass."

"Sister Busby." Stone's voice came through loud and clear through the Beta-Hummer's radio, which shocked its occupants back into the here and now. "I'm going ahead to reconnoiter the area. I'll check in every few minutes. Out."

"Where did he go?" Hassan said.

"There!" Reissen pointed. "I am following his footprints in the sand along the base of that cliff."

Hassan then spoke for them all. "Just who *is* this American?"

Reissen whispered, "One damn brave man. May God go with him."

*   *   *

Stone admitted to himself that being loose again in his Urban Combat Suit felt wonderful. The environmental fans were keeping him comfortable as he slowly stalked along the sand at the cliff's base looking for something, somewhere ahead. Only now could he feel the highly-agitated, totally pissed off attitude of something big and primal. Unconsciously, the Texan compared the feeling to one particular Brahma bull that lorded over his father's north pasture. The Lictor of Magic also tipped his hat to the Austrian. Erik had sensed this vibe way before he had. *That dude is one powerful sensitive. He just needs to lighten up some.*

Stone sensed, more than felt, a subtle vibration in the sand which stopped him dead in his tracks. Slowly, carefully, he got down on one knee, listened, and reached out with *all* of his senses. Then he saw it—the mostly buried and tilted remains of a small pickup truck. Looking around the rest of the depression with its high and steep cliff walls, he then noticed a small exposed rocky surface that to his eyes seemed all too flat. *That's probably the top of the structure. But what's protecting it and where?* So he tried the obvious. He started to call to it, but was stopped.

**Soul carrier. Your instincts are correct. But go slow with this one. It is not used to casual conversation with mortals. It's intelligent, can sense honesty, but is child-like and extremely proud. So repeat your respect for it many times.** So whispered the First Soul of Creation to its mortal carrier—Stone.

Closing his eyes and focusing, Stone psychically called out, *Oh mighty Kur, we mean you and your gate no harm.*

That psychic statement caused an audible stirring, a grating sound, from the deep sand beneath the ruined truck some one hundred feet away.

*Oh mighty Kur, we come in peace to study your gate, not to harm it.*

In response the truck's angle shifted slightly from the movement beneath it.

*Oh mighty Kur, we come in peace to study your gate, not to harm it.*

**Who dares address me by Name!**

The psychic impact of that response staggered Stone enough that he fell back onto his backside.

Righting himself, Stone continued. *Oh mighty Kur, I am the Lictor of Magic, and the carrier of the First Soul of Creation. We wish to study your gate in order to better protect it.*

**Lictor of Magic, carrier of the First Soul of Creation, *I* protect the Gate of the Netherworld! It is *my* purpose!**

*Oh mighty Kur, we come as friends. Allow us to study your gate, so that we may assist you.*

**I have no friends!**

*Oh mighty Kur, you do with us. The Devourer of Souls, he who thinks he rules the Dark Realm, hates me, despises me. I have wronged him and his minions many times.*

**Yesss ... I see that indeed you have ... Lictor of Magic, carrier of the First Soul. You deeply vex him and his subjects. That pleases me.**

*Oh mighty Kur, I beg you to return to your place of slumber. Allow us to study your gate and learn how to protect it.*

**You wish to do this ... why?**

*Oh mighty Kur, to prevent other ignorant mortals from doing mischief to it, thereby disturbing you, and threatening your purpose. You have my word as my bond.*

**Lictor of Magic, carrier of the First Soul, I know of your many deeds. The Ledger Keeper has shared them with me. I now see the righteousness in your heart. I will return to my place of watchfulness. You and yours may study what you wish.**

Once again the sand rasped loudly indicating the passage of something huge, and in so doing, the truck disappeared into a sandy eddy, almost like a scene plucked right out of the movie *Dune,* when a spice crawler vanished in a sandy vortex.

Letting out a deep sigh, Stone keyed this radio. "Sister Josephina."

"Stone! Are you all right?"

"Yes ma'am, I am. Dr. Reissen, sir, you are one powerful sensitive. Give me about five minutes to finish my reconnoiter, then I'll return with a full report. Out."

This I did, ever so gingerly, stepping forward with the cat's feet of a Carl Sandburg poem, my sword out and at the ready, expecting anything, but encountering nothing. Why I did so, I don't really know. I suppose having the Bone Sword out and in my hands gave me a sense of security—no matter how false it might have been. As for Kur, the guardian of the Netherworld's gate, it had kept its word. It was no longer present.

*   *   *

Stone made his return known by opening up our Hummer's tailgate. Its loud squeak caused all of us to jump, but I was heartily relieved to see Mr. J.J. back, and in one piece. Looking into the rearview mirror, he again performed his magic trick, but this time in reverse—first his head appeared as if floating in mid-air, then his well-muscled torso, and finally the rest. Within mere moments, Stone had all his gear stowed away. The tailgate closed with a crash and he got into our Hummer.

Only then did I see the dark rings of exhaustion around the man's eyes.

"That was some negotiation," Stone said.

Sister Busby—ever a bundle of nervous energy, said, "Tell us all about it," and then realized that Inspector Hassan was present. She quickly amended, "Sometime appropriate."

"You got it," Stone answered.

Hassan however, was not to be denied. "Mr Stone, just *how* did you do whatever you just did?"

"It's easy inspector, my high-tech suit is the latest in combat camouflage. It literally mimics its surroundings. Would you like to try it on yourself?"

"Yes, I would very much like that." Then, "Is it permitted?"

"Only *if* you tell no one about it, the suit is still highly classified by the US military." While the inspector beamed, Stone glanced meaningfully to Reissen and Sister Busby. He had managed to deflect the inspector's curiosity from matters far more grave.

# CHAPTER 14

After a brief conversation with Stone, Reissen delivered an abbreviated version to the rest of the team.

"First rule, hard and fast, no one touches the structure with anything metallic, period. If anything, the only tool permissible is either a short-handled sweep or broom. Absolutely *no* exceptions. Clear?" Reissen said firmly.

All of the archaeological team nodded like bobble-headed dolls, including Stone. Then Reissen thought to add, "Survey team. Be sure to heavily pad all of your equipment and stadia. I know that you will feel some accuracy will be lost. This is a preliminary investigation—not a full-blown excavation. Besides, your highly practiced skills will make up for this minor imprecision. Else, be sure to capture the surrounding environment and the structure as is. For the moment, that will do as well."

"Now let's start by clearing the roof and excavating the southwestern corner facing the ancient pavement. That would be the logical place for an entranceway. If anyone comes across any cultural remains—be it artwork, inscriptions, or artifacts, immediately stop what you are doing and get me."

Roth and Sister Busby began the laborious task of sweeping off the structure's flat roof. Wald joined them once her landscape photography was complete. Meanwhile, the rest of the crew focused on the southwestern corner. For them, it was truly grunt work stripping away literally cubic meters of sand. Their initial goal was to expose the southwestern corner to its footing just to get an idea of how tall the sloped red granite structure was.

Working with short-handled trenching hoes with their edges heavily duct taped, Reissen, Stone, Peters, and Franks formed a conga line next to one another while Hassan looked on. Digging "doggie style," they threw sand out from between their legs at a furious rate. Then, when a sufficient amount had been removed, the specific gravity of the sand above would slip down and apparently ruin their efforts, but in the process revealed a portion of the structure's upper sloped surface.

"I think this is a massive mastaba," Reissen decided.

"What's a mastaba?" Stone asked between shovelfuls.

"A flat-topped structure with sloped sides. The term mastaba itself is Arabic for 'mud brick bench'." Reissen explained. "See the analogy?"

"Yeah."

The four men endured four full sand slips before they exposed the fine upper-most groove of a plugged entranceway. While encouraging, Reissen drove them on, and after two more sand slippages, he called for a halt to assess the situation and to hydrate. By this time, the women above had swept off half of the structure's flat roof, which now took on the appearance of a vast, red, billiard table.

Gathering the team together, the archaeologist noted everyone's sweat stains, the effort that they had made, and on the spot made an executive decision.

"Today, we have made good progress. It's nearly noon and we're working in the high sun without shade. So finish drinking your liter of water. I am calling a halt for the day. Prepare to head back. Inspector Hassan has already called ahead with our needs. Tonight we stay in Memphis with our colleagues of the Austrian archaeological mission. Remember that we are only performing a preliminary investigation on the behalf of the Egyptian Antiquities Service. Nothing more." The Austrian stopped to lock eyes with everyone.

"And as for Mr. J.J., he is just an American Sumerologist who wants to experience the many romantic glories of Egyptian archaeology."

Chuckles broke out as Stone looked down at his sweat-drenched t-shirt. "Yep, just like Indiana Jones," the Texan said with a broad grin.

After a brief pause, Reissen continued, "Are we clear?"

All nodded in consent, even if they didn't fully understand why Reissen was asking for their discretion.

*   *   *

This time Busby, Roth, Reissen, and Stone rode back together in the Alpha-Hummer, following behind the Beta driven by Franks.

Once they got underway, Busby turned around in the passenger's seat and confronted Stone, "Okay, mister. What happened out there this morning? No secrets, we're all sensitives. We can tell if you're holding anything back."

"Oooo, the Spanish Inquisition! What's next? The comfy chair? A down pillow perhaps?" Stone quipped with a smirk.

Then the American looked her in the eye and said, "I psychically called to the primordial, using its

Sumerian name, and had a conversation. I assured it we meant no harm to the structure it guarded, and we were here to study and protect it. It took some negotiation, but in the end, it returned to its lair."

"What did you negotiate?" Sister Josephina pressed.

"What I just told you, nothing more."

"Did you see anything?"

"No, but I did feel and hear the sand grate as it moved about in the sand beneath an old truck, which disappeared."

"Jesus Christ Stone! You gave your word to a *demon*," Busby blurted out.

"It was hardly a demon, Sister Busby. It *is* however the primordial guardian of the Gate to the Netherworld. Its job is to prevent demons and dark souls from escaping into the Mortal Realm."

"How do you know that for sure?" the fiery red-headed nun pressed.

"Because it hates the Devourer of Souls as much as I."

Throughout this entire exchange, Reissen realized as never before why *The Knot of Eternity* had been required reading back at the Vatican. The unimaginable contents of that text had come alive right before his very eyes, and that fact alone he found unsettling. Here, his good friend from the Vatican and this remarkable American were discussing the relationship between the Netherworld's Gate Keeper and the Devourer of Souls—the dark master of that realm and its many demonic denizens, as if they were characters in a soap opera! Above all, to him at least, Stone seemed to be holding back a lot. If not asked directly about something, Stone kept his mouth shut and profile low.

Hearing that, the nun sat back on her heels and stared into the backseat. "How much contact with the Devourer of Souls have you had, Lictor of Magic?" She asked accusingly.

"None directly," Stone said with an easy shrug, "but I have sure sent my fair share of ruined demonkind its way. So indirectly, it definitely knows of me. Silver leaves a mark on a demon, and that's my trademark."

"Is there anything else you have been in congress with from the other side?"

"Yes, Sister Busby, for starters I carry the First Soul of Creation," that brought a quick gasp. "And I have had several conversations with the Ledger Keeper."

"You *do* get around, Mr. Stone," Sister Busby finally remarked as she turned to sit down.

Much like Reissen, Roth sat speechless. Everything she had ever learned about the cosmology of *The Knot of Eternity* was shockingly becoming true. Since Sheila first met Stone, she detected absolutely no guile or dishonesty. If anything, Stone came across as a consummate, if tight-lipped, professional, who was out on a job. In her eyes, the man was a stone-cold demon slayer, pure and simple.

\*   \*   \*

The team, with Inspector Hassan, started early the next day, just as dawn broke in a blinding glare. Deep within the depression, however, all remained shaded, cool and pleasant with a gentle breeze from the open desert. But everyone knew that would change quickly.

"So team, we continue where we left off yesterday," Reissen began. "Be mindful of dehydration. Above all, take care with your tools, and stop to rest when you need to."

With no appreciable wind during the night, the sweeping crew started where they left off on the structure's roof. After two more sand slides the digging crew had exposed the fine grooving of the entire entrance—complete with several smallish chips in its otherwise pristine outline.

"I suspect," Stone observed to Reissen, "it was those three chips that cost the two men their lives. Damn shame."

*"Wait!"* Reissen said nearly choking while he pointed with a quivering finger. "I see an inscription."

The Egyptologist was correct. Calling for a short-handled sweep, Reissen began vigorously brushing away at the red granite slope. Sand had lodged in the sharply carved hieroglyphs, which ran horizontally across the center of the entrance way's plug and beyond in both directions.

"It looks like one continuous frieze!" the Austrian giddily gibbered.

"In other words, Dr. Reissen, what you're saying is we have to dig out this entire structure. Correct?"

"I am truly sorry gentlemen, but I think Mr. J.J. is right."

This realization brought on some glazed looks as eyes scanned the length of just the southern side, which looked to be about ninety feet long.

Then with an infectious smile, Stone said. "Look at it this way guys," with his arms extended wide, "we have exclusive permission to study this monument.

Let's tackle it. Because I'm real curious as to what this inscription is all about."

For that matter, Reissen was too, but was thankful for Mr. J.J.'s enthusiastic support.

Later that day, as the two Hummers made their way back toward Memphis, Stone asked Reissen a sensitive question. "Erik, when are you going to let the rest of the team in on what we're excavating?"

Looking into his rearview mirror, the Austrian replied, "Tonight, Mr. J.J., after dinner."

*　*　*

Seven sated and relaxed individuals gathered around a picnic table under a breathtakingly starry night, where the Milky Way was clearly in evidence. Each, courtesy of Stone, was presented with a frosty cold half liter of Egyptian Stella beer. Several immediately took long, appreciative swigs, but Peters did not.

"Erik. I do not like this. Why are you trying to soften us up?" the surveyor said with accusing eyes focused upon the blond-haired American.

"Most adroit of you, Jürgen. The whole idea of the beer was Mr. J.J.'s. And I do indeed wish to share some bad news with you. Just hear me out. That is all. Then, afterward, we can discuss whether to proceed or not. Fair?"

Nods came from everyone. Peters sat there with crossed arms. His beer untouched.

"First of all, this is a preliminary investigation into an unknown structure. Its purpose is to positively ascertain what that red granite structure is. Our current hypothesis is that it is the physical Gate to the Netherworld."

The collective jaws of Peters, Franks, and Wald dropped as one.

"Furthermore, Mr. J.J. here is on loan to this team from a secular paranormal organization, while Sheila, Sister Josephina, and I represent the Vatican's interests."

Wald asked, "Erik, what precisely do you mean by 'the physical Gate to the Netherworld'?"

"Just that, Else. The Netherworld, Hades, Hell in our terms, is an actual place. It is guarded by a gate keeper to prevent demons and dark souls from escaping. This gate keeper also defends this gate like a possessive and hyperactive pit bull. This is why I have absolutely prohibited any metallic contact with the monument's red granite exterior. Such scrapes would enrage it into thinking we are somehow damaging it.

This is why our short trenching shovels are wrapped in duct tape. Why Jürgen's and Willi's equipment are similarly padded.

"Now," the Austrian leaned in, "I know this is a lot to digest. So I would like everyone to sleep on it. Tomorrow morning before breakfast I want to hear from each of you individually and in private, regarding if you wish to continue with this investigation or not."

Not surprisingly, the beers of Franks, Wald, and Peters were left unfinished. Reissen and Stone saw this as a good sign. The threesome were taking this seriously.

The next morning, the survey team bowed out on the grounds that their work was complete. Wald did as well. Privately, Reissen was greatly relieved by their cautious decisions. In many respects, he had felt guilty requesting their help and leveraging their friendship. From here on out, the rest of this "preliminary investigation" would to be shouldered solely by the paranormal professionals.

*   *   *

Two days later, Stone and Reissen, with the help of Roth and Busby, had denuded the entire southern side of the "monument," as it came to be known. With its flat roof also swept clean, it took on the look of a magnificent red granite jewel with freakishly smooth facets. As for its longitudinal inscription, Reissen had this to say about it at the end of day four.

"Well, I have some good news. The inscription is not continuous, but rather repetitive. That means that we do not have to dig out the entire structure." That announcement brought on a flood of relieved sighs.

"In the broadest of terms, the gist of the inscription is a dire warning not to approach, touch, or desecrate it in any manner. Along with that warning is a threat that anyone who does so will be 'struck down.' When I have a reasonable translation, I will share it. Tomorrow I make a request for a final survey and photo shoot. While not absolutely required, I will still make a plea tonight. For now, even though it is early, let's pack up and return to Memphis."

"Not quite yet Erik," Stone said in a rare moment of opposition while he gazed up at the northern cliffs.

Used to having his own way in all things archaeological, Reissen, bristled and asked, "Why?"

"Because my dear colleague, there is something to explore near the base of that cliff."

Now turning around, the Austrian said, "Where, Mr. J.J.?"

"See that crack over there? I'll just bet you one icy cold beer that it isn't a crack."

"Done." The crew followed the thirst-motivated archaeologist toward the rocky cliff face. After picking their way through the scree at its base, the Egyptologist was shocked at what he saw. Cleverly concealed within the fissure's shadow was an artificially smoothed field. The chisel marks were clearly evident. Relieved into the rock was fashioned a beautifully preserved false door—an ancient Egyptian magical portal carved to mimic a house door, its lintel, and an image of the deceased with an offering slab before it. Surrounding it, ten vertical registers of hieroglyphs listed the deceased biographical information along with formulaic spells.

As the foursome gathered around to gape, the delighted Austrian whispered, "Well, Mr. J.J., I owe you a beer," as his fingers traced over the finely cut hieroglyphics in delicate raised relief. But as he did so, a frown formed.

"Now this is an odd name. It's definitely not Egyptian."

"What's it say?" Stone impatiently pushed.

> May Osiris bestow an offering of bread,
> beer, oxen, birds, alabaster, clothing, and
> every good and pure thing upon the high
> priest and seer of *Nmm, Gskm.*

> For the *ka* of the revered high priest and
> seer *Gskm*, true of voice, son of the
> trader *Nrgl*, and weaver *Shhm*, from the
> land of the Two Rivers, high praise is
> bestowed by Imhotep, master architect
> and magician to the Horus, *Net-jeri-khet
> Djoser.*

> The devotion, wisdom, and energy of the
> Venerable *Gskm* has made the Red and
> Black lands of *Kemet* secure for millions
> of years. May his *ka* endure. May his *ka*
> journey safely through the many gates of
> the Netherworld to a place most pleasing.

"*Mein Gott!* The owner of this false door, a man
called *Gskm*, was a high priest of a goddess named
*Nmm*, from a city in the land between the Two Rivers!"

Stone blurted out, "That's Nammu, a Sumerian
creator goddess, and this goddess's patron city in the
land between the Two Rivers was none other than Ur!"

"You must be right Mr. J.J., for his father's and
mother's names, *Nrgl* and *Shhm*, are not Egyptian
names either."

"Those names look Sumerian in origin," Stone
confirmed.

As Reissen continued to translate the inscription,
he shook his head from side to side in wonderment.
"Mr. J.J., it seems that this *Gskm* was very well
connected. I bet you one icy cold beer that the Imhotep

mentioned in this inscription built this funerary monument for him."

The Texan just smiled. "You're on."

Then, "There's something else amiss," Roth observed, "the traditional magical offering known as the *htp-di-nsw* formula, or 'the offering given by the king,' is entirely missing."

Hand to his chin, Reissen said, "Yes Sheila, so it is. But if *Gskm* is Sumerian, as we suspect, I seriously doubt that such a traditional Egyptian offering would apply."

\* \* \*

As had become habit, Reissen drove the lone Hummer back to Memphis. The transit had become a mostly silent and melancholy one, but today, once underway, Stone bluntly asked the Egyptologist, "Erik, what's your impression of the false door's paleography?"

"Definitely pre-Fourth Dynasty as the name Imhotep was mentioned. The composition is that of a master scribe—extremely literate and precise. The artistic craftsmanship of the glyphs is superb. That alone indicates much, as in noble or royal connections. As to why a Sumerian priest deserved such a monument that overlooked the Gate to the Netherworld is highly significant. It almost seems like he was somehow involved with the monument. That would be my preliminary guess."

"Fine and dandy, but what's your read on the gate's inscription?" Stone probed.

"Mr. J.J., I have been struggling with that question. It predates the Classical Egyptian hieroglyphs of the Middle Kingdom. It even contains a handful of glyphs that I do not recognize. In addition, its grammar is awkward, as if a young scribe had composed it, instead of a master. Then there are several anachronisms that suggest Archaic or earlier constructions. It is nothing like the composition of the false door. In fact, it is a polar opposite."

"So chronologically, what's your preliminary guess?"

"Oh, do not quote me, but right now I would say somewhere between Dynasty Zero and the Third Dynasty."

A long pause ensued as Stone stared out the window at the now all too familiar landscape that passed before him. Then he asked, "Erik, is it possible the inscription was composed by a foreign speaker, someone for whom Egyptian was a second language?"

The archaeologist glanced in his rearview mirror at Stone with a frown. "Where are you fishing, Mr. J.J.?"

"Well, from my point-of-view, the name of the gate's guardian is Sumerian. The Gate Keeper readily responded to it, yet nowhere in the repetitive inscription is it specifically mentioned. Now we have a monument of a Sumerian priest overlooking the gate. I well know the names of powerful magical entities rarely appear on public monuments. But beyond that caveat, I know you have observed an almost careless quality to the inscription's construction, along with several odd glyphs. Could it be that a Sumerian wrote that warning, trying his best to translate his words into understandable Egyptian?"

A light bulb went off in Reissen's head. "And that could perhaps explain the odd grammar as well. Mr. J.J., I think that you may be on to something!"

\* \* \*

That evening after dinner, two linguists—one an Egyptologist and the other a Sumerologist, put their collective heads together.

"How do you propose we start?" Reissen asked.

"My suggestion would be to begin with a straight transliteration of the gate's inscription. If there is any

Sumerian in it, I'll be able to spot it. If that fails, then we'll have to tackle the grammar of the message itself. That may betray something as well, perhaps the hint of a Sumerian mindset."

Reissen grunted his approval, and off they went.

In the process, Stone lubricated the effort with several frosty half-liter bottles of Stella beer. Instead of crippling Reissen's mind, Stone saw it open up like a wondrous flower. *Damn. This guy's good. Too bad Mr. Good never met him. Talk about two peas in a pod.*

*   *   *

"J.J.," as Reissen decided to call me after polishing off several of my beers, "I need to explain the bibliography on early hieroglyphs. Unlike what goes on in your field with periodic updates and revisions based on the latest archaeological finds, we in Egyptology have to make do with very outdated publications. This situation is all the more so when we try to decipher early hieroglyphic inscriptions."

Reissen then spun his laptop around to share its screen. "Look here my friend. The first pioneer in the field was Hilda Petrie in 1927. That means her source material dated to what was known prior to then—in the main museum and special collections' material. While useful, you can imagine how outdated it is today.

"During the late thirty's Walter Emery was digging at Sakkara. In the process, he really accelerated our understanding of early hieroglyphs. Not only did he find many early inscriptions, he could date them as well, because his sandbox included the tombs of Egypt's First and Second Dynasty kings. Consequently for the field, his work represented a quantum leap forward.

"The next worthwhile source for archaic hieroglyphs is dated to 1963 with Peter Kaplony's work. In many respects, his compilation was merely a convenient catalogue of what was known at the time. He provided nothing new. Sadly, his work is the most recent treatment on the subject.

"However, we are in luck, for the glyphs that I did not recognize were represented in Emery's excavation reports and Kaplony's book. Let's face facts. Emery was primarily an archaeologist, while Kaplony was a philologist. But Kaplony in many instances made sense of what Emery had found."

"So what you're saying Erik, is that you're afraid you might be shooting in the dark with antiquated information?" I asked. "J.J.," the Egyptologist said with a shake of his head, "This analysis will be sketchy at best."

"Understood. But nothing ventured, nothing gained."

\* \* \*

And did we ever venture—*far*. I blame J.J. entirely for this exercise as I was not comfortable building an argument based on suppositions. But damn it all, the fragile structure we built hung together.

So what did J.J. and I come up with? Remarkably, not one, but two messages lurked within the same inscription. On the one hand, we had an archaic Egyptian text, grammatically crude, but understandable. On the other, once we transliterated the Egyptian, there lay, lo' and behold, a Sumerian subtext that addressed the Gate Keeper of the Netherworld, Kur, by name, and tersely warned off all that approached.

As far as I was concerned, this result represented a tremendous breakthrough from several points-of-view. For both the false door and the monument's ancient inscriptions provided proof positive of early Mesopotamian cultural influence on the Nile Valley. Additionally, a long-held academic thesis was enhanced—the notion that written language emanated outward from the land between the two rivers to the Nile Valley. But the real question remained—who built it?

The unfortunate fact that I faced was that the answer came from the Sumerian priest's false door, an inscription that would never be allowed to reach the light of day. So too, with the gate's inscription, because to do so would admit the existence of something that normals would go mad over—a physical gate that led to the Netherworld. Not good.

\*   \*   \*

Fortunately, Wald, Franks, and Peters agreed to one last stint at the "preliminary investigation" site to record both the remains in the north cliff face and the gate.

"Erik," Peters reported, "the dimensions of the monument are very curious, very deliberate."

"How so Jürgen?"

"Its rectangular ground plan is eighty-nine feet by fifty-five, fashioned with stone blocks the size of train cars. That calculates to fifty-two by thirty-two Egyptian cubits—the exact ratio of a golden rectangle."

*"Mein Gott!"*

"In fact, the calculation comes out as 1.6181818 into infinity. And there's more. While Willi and I measured out the entranceway, we discovered its dimensions possessed that ratio as well. But it doesn't end there. That entranceway is a dummy. It's just an outline—a groove that was uniformly cut only four inches deep."

"How did you determine that?" Reissen asked.

"Willi used a broom straw."

The Egyptologist let out a deep sigh. "Thank you Jürgen."

At that moment, Stone walked up to him and said, "Why the glum face Erik?"

"That entrance is a dummy J.J. It's just for show. Basically, it is a poor imitation of an Egyptian false door."

"That may be, Erik, but two men died believing that it was the real thing."

"J.J., do we even dare look for an entrance?"

"Frankly, I wouldn't," the north Texan said. "I'd let sleeping dogs lie. Besides, are you willing to chance troubling the Gate Keeper?"

"No, of course not. But J.J., why have such an artifice to begin with?"

"To deceive the ignorant away from the true purpose of the structure—it's a cork in the ultimate bottle." Stone stated. "This was built to look like a mastaba-shaped cenotaph, pure and simple. End of story. Its true purpose had to be camouflaged if it were ever discovered."

# CHAPTER 15

Pulling gees loads not normally recommended, the mission crew of *Kamakazi One* didn't care one wit as their vehicle sprinted on a continuous burn into deep space. Locked on an intercept course with the asteroid Gravitron, their operational plan could not have been clearer—get out there quick, launch, and then run like hell and hide.

The mission crew of four—two men and two women—left families behind for this daring ride. All former military, Jarvis' theory for selecting them was about reliability and motivation. If successful, their families would never again need for anything. If all went according to plan, their heavily shielded command module would save their lives. As for the module itself, it looked like a kid's glider model complete with its own reentry and attitude rockets. All sincerely hoped for a leisurely return trip home, but none seriously expected it.

\*  \*  \*

"Mission Control Vandenberg, this is *K-1*. Sixty seconds to launch. Over."

"Roger, *K-1*."

That was the first and only scheduled transmission since *Kamakazi One*'s launch. It was thought best to keep the chatter down to a minimum for operational security. Even though their transmissions were heavily encrypted, someone could still theoretically place a fix on their location.

Mission Commander Josie Brown wiped the sweat from her forehead one last time before she donned and sealed her helmet. "Listen up everyone," she said over their helmet communications feed. "Seal up. Prepare for launch and evasive maneuvers."

She heard three immediate acknowledgments.

Mission Specialist Jonathan Tiggs sat impassively with his hand near the launch trigger and guidance mechanism. He waited for Brown's countdown and command to launch the Raptor, which carried the nuclear device.

Mission Specialist Molly Gunther manned the radar and navigation console. She was the next to break the tense silence. "Sixty kilometers to target. Closing rapidly. Recommend commencement of countdown on my mark ... Mark."

"Countdown initiated." Brown said as she punched in the clock and buttons that released the locks on the rocket's hard point moorings.

Mission Pilot Doug Rizzo held the vehicle steady with both his hands on the steering controls. Unbidden, his thoughts wandered briefly to his high school days of playing an old video game called *Asteroids*.

Rizzo heard Brown beginning the countdown.

"Ten.

"Nine.

"Eight.

"Seven.

"Six.

"Five.

"Four.

"Three.

"Two.

"One.

"Launch."

Leaving the moorings of their mission vehicle with a mild shake, the Raptor sped away—its engine a glowing sun. "Launch confirmed," Tiggs reported. "Raptor running true."

"Initiate evasive maneuvers," Brown coolly ordered.

Rizzo responded by triggering the main engine. The plan called for the command module to get behind the asteroid before the detonation, to hide within its shadow.

"Lord, get us safely beyond that sucker!" Gunther prayed from her navigation station.

"Raptor continues to run true," Tiggs inserted into the heavy silence.

"Helmet blast shields *down!*" Brown ordered.

"Detonation imminent," Tiggs unnecessarily added.

Even through the heavy visors, all saw a blinding burst of intense light. That it didn't flood the module's cabin was a tribute to Rizzo's maneuvering. The pilot had cut the module's main engine just as the craft slid into the asteroid's shadow with its heavily shielded ass-end facing the blast. His timing could not have been better.

"Gravitron took the hit hard," Gunther gleefully confirmed from her radar. "It's breaking up. I count six fragments and a shitload of debris."

The crew cheered and hooted as one. Brown called out over the din, "Good shooting Tiggs! I want you on my next bird hunt!"

"And damn fine flying Mr. Rizzo," Brown softly added. "Now get us home."

"Yes ma'am. Gunther, get me a plot around that debris cloud. You're now our eyes."

"I'm on it!"

Meanwhile, Mission Commander Brown settled herself down to compose her report. "Mission Control Vandenberg. *K-1* reports six fragments. Repeat. Six fragments. Over."

"Roger, *K-1*. We confirm six fragments. Job *well done.*"

Brown could clearly hear the boisterous cheering in the background of Vandenberg's transmission.

\*   \*   \*

Master Sergeant Gene Roberts once again had a lot on his mind as he rubbed at the bristles of his chin. He had been monitoring the spectacular breakup of Gravitron for the past ten hours straight. A natural-born worrier, he purposely settled in to track the fragments. In the twelfth hour of his self-imposed exile, one of the fragments began to trouble him. Careening wildly in an unpredictable fashion, he patiently watched it from his station deep within the Colorado mountain fortress. It troubled him.

* * *

The entire event was reported in the evening news as the miraculous impact of two asteroids in deep space. The threat of a near-Earth encounter with a planet-killer had been averted by the whimsy of celestial mechanics. A worldwide "all clear" joyously echoed around the planet. Places of worshipped filled to capacity. Crowds spontaneously gathered in streets to celebrate. And yes, there were even reports of several mindless few who burned cars and rioted.

The successful return of *Kamakazi One*, however, went completely unnoticed and by design. The plan called for its glide path to end at Vandenberg, but because of fuel depletion due to the craft's wide skirting of the debris cloud, *K-1* was diverted to Denver International. This caused the security weenies to piss their pants. Nearby Buckley AFB would have been a better choice, but its runways were too short. So it was Denver, which suited Rizzo just fine. That was where he called home.

Landing and rolling to a stop, only then did the module's crew remove their helmets with loud sighs of relief. Why? Because Brown discovered that the integrity of the cabin's atmosphere had been compromised by who knows how many debris impacts.

"Let's get the hell out!" Tiggs said while furiously unbuckling his eight-point harness.

"Not so fast cowboy. This rig is hot as shit out there. Or are you just that crazy?" Rizzo jabbed. "Relax. Take a nap, while this fine piece of Jarvis Industries know-how cools its heels."

While Rizzo was busy schooling Tiggs on the realities of atmospheric friction, DIA's emergency crews surrounded the hot fuselage of the command module like a herd of buffalo protecting their calves. One supervisor dared to approach, but all too soon backed off and got on his radio.

"Stay back everyone! You can fry an egg on that sucker!"

By the time the command module had cooled down sufficiently to open its two hatches, the security weenies from Buckley AFB had shooed away DIA's emergency ground crews and replaced them with their own.

Tiggs was the first to emerge and Brown was the last. As the others were led off by an arm to a mobile emergency van, Brown shrugged off the assistance to inspect the module's fuselage. While not noticeable from the nose or two sides, the rear of the craft was absolutely peppered with holes. Rizzo had done good.

Meanwhile, in the USAF medical wagon, a medical corpsman scanned the crew, smiled, and declared, "Only three x-rays worth of RADS from the dentist's office. You lucky folks are good to go."

The future of Jarvis Industries was forever assured.

*    *    *

A day later, the Joint Chiefs made a quiet visit to the Oval Office to meet with their president. When they entered, POTUS stood up from his desk. The seven took seats on the two couches that had been turned to face him. The traditional coffee table had disappeared. The subliminal message: no hospitality today. The president didn't even bother to sit down as he addressed them.

"Gentlemen. The planet has just been saved by the agility, ingenuity, and know-how of a private-held American corporation. Granted, we supplied them with the device and its delivery system. Granted, we opened up Vandenberg for their launch. But they did the rest. But we must do better. Consider," he emphasized with an upraised finger, "bureaucracy almost killed this planet."

Grim and sober faces ringed the conference table. The Commander-in-Chief looked each in the eye before he continued. His delivery was quiet, but there was a certain tremble to it that was unmistakable.

"That fact, gentlemen, is unexceptable. I don't care what it takes, I don't care whose cow is gored, I *certainly* don't care about tradition. I want the Pentagon slimmed down—drastically. What I want, gentlemen, is an agile and efficient Pentagon that can turn on a *dime,* instead of aimlessly wallowing about like a pregnant buffalo."

The president paused, looked down at some notes, and continued.

"To this very day, I know of nothing in our strategic or tactical arsenals that is ready to go like the Jarvis spacecraft. This nation deserves something useful, practical, and available at a moment's notice. Have I made myself clear?"

Seven nods silently answered, but one, the Air Force general, had a faraway look in his eyes that the president didn't miss. As they stood as one to leave, the president asked the general for a private moment.

"Yes, Mr. President?"

"General Cooks, what do you have up your sleeve?"

"Sir?"

"General, I'm no fool. If you were playing poker, you left behind one hell of a big tell. What is it that the Air Force has, or has in development, that can match *Kamakazi One*?"

The general looked down at his shiny shoes to consider his response and then said, "Mr. President, *that* development has been an ongoing process since the late 1940's."

"Fine. Wonderful. But when is this *thing* going to be operational?"

"Its operational testing is scheduled two months from now."

"*Testing*, you say. Just how ready, right now, is this multi-generational *toy* of yours?"

Now looking the occupant of the Oval Office straight in the eye. "It could have flown yesterday, Mr President. It could have delivered that package. But its successful return remained in doubt."

"Just so I understand you general. Your service just got beat out by a biplane, while you were unwilling to put in a questionably airworthy fighter jet harm's way. Is that correct?"

"Mr. President, that analogy is not fair. We have invested so much time and money . . ."

Now interrupting, "Not fair? General, global extinction is not fair either."

Then, suddenly, the president remembered his telepathic conversation with Betsy Silver Moon, closed his eyes, and saw into the general's mind. And what he saw amazed him.

Now opening his eyes, he said, "So general, why the triangular profile?"

"Wha-ttt?" the general stuttered.

"I'll just bet that airframe is pretty quiet isn't it, general? Maybe even the last word in stealth technology."

"Mr. President, I cannot ..."

"I know general, but just in case you have forgotten, I am the Commander-in-Chief."

\*  \*  \*

"Betsy," Dr. Shinto began her voicemail, "you can stand down whatever plans you devised to address the NEO. It has been destroyed. We're safe. Bye."

Silver Moon paused to let out a deep and cleansing sigh at hearing that good news. Then, impulsively, she got an idea, picked up her phone, glanced at her wristwatch, made a quick calculation, and placed an international call to Rome.

"President Silver Moon, what a pleasant surprise," William DeSalvo, the chairman of CMES said. "What can I possibly do for you?"

"Chairman DeSalvo, I wish to first, once again, thank you for your six volunteers. However, I have been just informed that the threat no longer exists. That it has been, somehow, destroyed."

"Ah yes, that providential celestial collision that everyone has been talking about. Is that what you are referring to?"

"Yes, but more importantly, I have learned something very important from this crisis that didn't happen. Don't you think that we should communicate and perhaps even meet on a regular basis?"

"President Silver Moon, I could not agree more."

# CHAPTER 16

Within the paranormal communities, the most commonly paid occupation is that of "tracker." Sensitives of all kinds fulfill this role. Lost your car keys? Call up a tracker. Your house was broken into and you want that precious necklace back. Contract a tracker. There are some undesirables you want to keep an eye on—get a tracker. And conceivably, trackers can track trackers as well. But the best trackers are culture-specific. They know the language(s), they intimately understand the environment, and they, much like chameleons, blend in perfectly. Gamal Safar was such a tracker.

Within modern Egyptian culture, *Baksheesh* is a traditional method of economic exchange for tips, charitable donations, and outright acts of corruption or bribery. It's the Egyptian way. Safar hid his psychic talents behind this institution like a mask. A master of gab and networking, the man could work a room all the while picking it clean of choice telepathic bits and pieces.

When Safar had been contracted to track down the specifics of a particular rumor, he made sure that he carried a wad of small bills in one pocket, while in the other a far more substantial amount. During his rounds he fully expected to run into his fair share of dead ends That was part and parcel of a tracker's job. Patience, persistence, taking note of body language, and listening with both his ears and mind were his greatest assets.

Because of the fantastic nature of the rumor, Safar began with an inquiry at the governmental offices of the Sakkaran Archaeological District. He did so going on a hunch, which for this man oftentimes was far better than a formal introduction.

His target was the district inspector, but the bureaucrat was not available. When Safar inquired about the inspector's whereabouts with his personal secretary, a vague look of disinterest passed across the man's face, which clearly indicated to Safar the need for financial lubrication. That accomplished, the tracker was told of a location near the Sakkaran Plateau. Pad at the ready, Safar took several notes and dawdled over them to indicate to the secretary the importance of his words and to phish for more detail. None, however, was forthcoming. As the tracker had already paid this greedy lackey enough, he moved on.

Safar's next stop took him to the Sakkaran police station—another hunch, where flashing a fake press ID, he bluffed his way all the way to a dispatch sergeant.

"Officer, I am researching a story about two missing men in the desert. I was told that your office handled the case. Can you be of any assistance?" The question was asked with a solicitous handshake and the deft passing of currency. After the officer openly inspected his gift, grunted his approval, and pocketed it, he said, "I am sorry, I cannot help you. That search was undertaken by a military security force out of Dhashur. It was their helicopter that found the missing truck." After some note taking, the "press man" thanked the officer profusely, moved on, and concluded that the dolt knew more than he divulged.

During the ten kilometer drive over to the Dhashur military base and airfield, Safar worked out his game plan. His ultimate target was the helicopter pilot who flew the search pattern and found the missing truck.

After only three minor investments, Safar hit the jackpot this time, and sat down opposite a helicopter pilot named Flight Lieutenant Mustafa El Mahdy.

"Lieutenant El Mahdy, thank you for agreeing to see me," the tracker began after parting with five hundred Egyptian pounds—his largest investment thus far. "I am an investigator hired by the missing men's family. They wish to find the whereabouts of their missing family members' bodies. I am quite sure you understand."

The veteran helicopter pilot indeed did, but he could also distinctly smell B.S. as easily as the next.

Sensing this reaction by the pilot, Safar smoothly transitioned from purely family matters and inquired directly, "While you were over the search area, did you happen to notice anything out-of-the-ordinary?"

To his surprise the pilot answered, "Why yes, I did. When we were on the ground, the place gave me an odd feeling, like I was being watched. And, there was of course the rectangle."

"Rectangle?" *What do we have here?*

"What do you mean lieutenant?" Safar inquired innocently, as he sat at the edge of his chair.

"There was a buried structure next to the victims' half-buried truck."

*Ignore the structure. Remain calm.*

"Do you know the coordinates of this half-buried truck?" the investigator asked hopefully, "So the family may recover it?"

"No longer. My superior passed them on to the inspector of the Sakkaran Archaeological District."

"Why did he do that?"

A shrug, "That is beyond my pay grade."

"I see. Would you happen to have saved a copy of them in your flight log?"

The answer was "yes," but the pilot did not like his interrogator. There was something distinctly, indefinably slimy about him. And, perhaps perversely, the pilot frankly did not want to divulge the coordinates.

"No sir. I am very sorry. But that flight log is over two weeks old, and so is long erased. It would be best to ask the Sakkaran archaeological inspector himself for what you seek. That's who my superior shared the flight log information with. That would be my best suggestion," the lieutenant said while trying to sound helpful.

As Safar left the military base he swore under his breath. "That officious little prick, he was sitting on that flight log all along and wouldn't share it. I could feel it." He made some notes nonetheless. "I could really use that information like right about now. My pockets are getting light."

The next stop for Safar was the Sakkaran Plateau. While a hunch, it was the manner in which the secretary at the archaeological office had described the location.

The tracker was certain his current vehicle would not be appropriate for where he had to go, but he had to make sure.

He drove on. The helicopter pilot had slipped the mention of the passing of two weeks. A lot can happen in that timeframe. On he searched, but Safar eventually found the agricultural secondary road that skirted along the base of the plateau. About a kilometer south of the famous Step Pyramid, there is was—a natural saddle in the plateau that led west into the desert. By his estimation, at least eight different sets of wide desert tracks left the secondary road and headed due west over a low rise and into the wastes. Consulting his smart device's GPS services, he noted down the coordinates. Tomorrow he would return better prepared.

*   *   *

The Discovery Land Rover was over sixteen years old, but Safar knew it well. He had gone overland in the stubborn all-terrain vehicle all the way to the Red Sea and back, several times. This little jaunt, at least in his mind, was a simple matter of driving slowly and avoiding notice. With his engine well-muffled, plenty of water, four spare jerry cans of petrol, and fresh sand tires, the tracker felt invincible. But before he set off, he made notice of the tire tracks once again. They were the same in number, but now more eroded by the wind. In another week's time, they were sure to disappear altogether. *Perfect,* he thought. *There is no indication that anyone is at the site.*

Shifting into low and revving the motor, he easily crested the ridgeline, and now just followed the tracks. As he drove into the wasteland, the more claustrophobic the route became with its surrounding rocky cliff sides. Finally, after rounding a gentle bend, a depression opened up before him and he came to a halt. Front and center someone had excavated one side and cleared off the rooftop of some sort of structure. Before he ventured into the depression, he took note of its coordinates on his device, and wrote them down in his notebook just to make sure.

Restarting the Discovery, he eased down into the depression, again following the tire tracks, and made his way over to the cleared area in the sand. For some reason, Safar did not immediately exit his vehicle. Instead he was satisfied with what he could see from behind the wheel and through his camera's viewfinder of his smart device. Once finished, he sent off the video, the passage's route, and the depression's coordinates, to his benefactor.

The tracker was about to pull out when he saw it—the outline edging of an entrance passage and a long inscription. Tantalized beyond all control, Safar dismounted and approached the entrance in the sloped red granite surface. Across its centerline ran a horizontal inscription that seemingly wrapped around the structure like a package string. There and then, he began another video, but this time from much closer range—barely inches away. He panned slowly to his right being sure to fill the screen with the beautifully cut hieroglyphs. He knew that his benefactor would appreciate this unexpected bonus. With measured, steady steps, he continued to video oblivious to his surroundings. Then, the unthinkable happened.

\*　　\*　　\*

The old witch of Barcelona received the email from her tracker, reviewed the video, and smiled a satisfied smile. She also knew how to keep her secrets safe. She sat back in the Queen Ann chair in her conjuring room and closed her eyes. Her hands moved in intricate patterns and lips whispered softly in a long lost archaic Latin dialect.

\*　　\*　　\*

Safar suddenly tripped and fell. In so doing, the tracker blundered against the red granite slope. His cevice carelessly dragged across its face with a loud metallic scraping sound that echoed off the nearby cliffs. For the Gate Keeper that was enough. Having fallen cn his right hip, a bolt of pain shot into Safar's brain, followed by the crucial question—*did I break something?*

The tracker sensed then distinctly heard a looming danger behind him – an electric presence. It began as a raw scraping, rasping sound of abraded sand. As Safar painfully rolled over on his back, he laid in a shadow cast by a nightmare. Twelve feet of thick, jet black belly scales extended from the sand and hovered above him. A large, narrow, and bird-like head with jade green eyes studied him like a laboratory specimen. A dark mouth opened filled with razor sharp teeth ready to strike. And as the horror did, its red feathery, plumage sprang erect in excitement along its head and spine. With remarkable speed, the beast struck Safar at the waist, sending an untold voltage of static electricity through him, arching his back in spasm, accompanied by an anguished scream.

The Gate Keeper sawed its jaws, and when it lifted its head, its scissor-like teeth had fully, cleanly, removed the tracker's lower torso. Raising its head like a bird, the Gate Keeper snapped its head back and swallowed the morsel whole in one gulp. It then fastidiously took, one by one, each of Safar's severed and still twitching legs in separate, almost dainty, bites. Bleeding out and pooling at a horrific rate, with the contents of his lower abdomen sagging out, the Gate Keeper bent over to look directly into the dying man's dilated eyes, his throat already hoarse from screaming.

**Mortal, you taste of demon! Why is that?**

Safar's head shook in open-mouthed silence in negation and total surrender.

Measuring carefully, the Gate Keeper unhinged its jaws, turned its head just so, and took the tracker whole from head to gut. At that point, Safar's final scream ended abruptly when his neck snapped like a twig. The tracker's last thought was, *By Allah's beard, the rumor was true!*

Finished with the perpetrator of its gate's defacement, the Gate Keeper returned to the sand, swirled deep beneath the Discovery, and sucked it down leaving no trace. Only a set of tire tracks remained, ending abruptly.

The entire event had been recorded by the still running device in a full 4G digital. It captured Safar's pitiful screams and entreaties, and much, much more.

\*    \*    \*

Moments later and several time zones away Safar's last moments had been felt, while his body and his eternal soul were rent asunder. The psychic pulse of that moment impacted the ancient witch of Barcelona, causing her to gasp. Swiftly getting under control she unnecessarily concluded, *it seems* Monsieur *Safar has passed on. He was such a personable man, but unfortunately such a dangerous loose end.*

Without another thought, the witch reread the email's concise contents. She smiled creating a hideous flood of laugh-lines across her face.

*Oh now I have you Lictor of Magic! Let's see what you do when the Gate of the Netherworld is breached! Who will you guard first? The Vatican? Old Oaks Academy? Or perhaps your rumored Alexandrian witch of a wife? I just can't wait to see this grand drama unfold!*

Her fingers then flew across the device's screen as she informed her two partners-in-crime of the good news. Afterward, she impulsively copied one set of coordinates from the email, pasted them into Google Earth, and was instantly transported from Barcelona's trendy La Boqueria market to the sands of Egypt's Western Desert.

*Oh my, I just love the way they do that!* The witch beamed at no one in particular, although several passersby did unconsciously glance in her direction at the witch's exuberant pulse of pleasure. Her screen panned up from Barcelona as if by rocket, traveled across the blue Mediterranean, and began its descent into the tan-colored Egyptian wastes. And there it was—a faint rectangle buried in the sands. Just seeing the gate from this God-like point-of-view caused ripples of excitement to again course through her millennium-plus body.

*And after all of this time, many had scoffed, but now I know it exists, and even better, know where. My dear Aubrey would have been so pleased at the news. Pity the Vatican had hunted him down like a mad dog. Under no circumstances did he deserve that.* Bitter loneliness now displaced the pleasure of her discovery.

\*   \*   \*

One of those casual passersby registered the old witch's emotional spike and likened its intensity to a fierce orgasm.

*At her age, I doubt it. That means that she's up to something. And knowing Portia Le Fey that something isn't good,* the Vatican tracker concluded.

Unfortunately for Justine D'Angelo, she had not been able to grasp the gist of Le Fey's jubilation, but her psychic antennae had definitely twitched. She had shadowed this witch and those other two crones off and on ever since the Barcelona coven had been laid low by TIIIS. If anything, reducing that snake pit from sixty-two to only three vipers had made her job considerably easier.

*     *     *

D'Angelo's field report was received by her supervisor with interest, especially given the specific window of time when the witch had read her device Such specificity focused the Vatican's search, which meant a faster understanding of that which might be critical.

The Jesuit priest sorted through several emails that the witch received that day and stopped dead on the one from Egypt. The middle-aged cleric shook his head in total shock at the unencrypted, yet highly sensitive content. *How can people operate like this in this day and age?* The content copied, he sent it immediately on to Cardinal Alberti, sure in the knowledge that he would know what best to do with it.

# CHAPTER 17

"Lieutenant Myers, I think we may have a problem." Master Sergeant Roberts concluded with a deep frown that wrinkled his receding hairline.

"You have my undivided sergeant. Now wow me."

"After three days of analysis, I found that one of the Gravitron fragments, specifically Fragment Four, has a mind of its own. It's trending along our orbital plane."

"No shit ... so how far out is this rogue asteroid?"

"Tracking says two AU and closing." Roberts sighed.

"What's Four's parameters?"

"It's no slouch, sir. It weighs in at 6.88 billion kilos and is 95.68 meters across. It's predicted near-Earth flyby is in eight months, give or take."

"How close?"

"That's where it gets real interesting. I spoke with Dr. Rohr about this, and it is her provisional opinion that Fragment Four is a planetary threat. Her provisional opinion is a Torino 6 to 8."

"Jesus. How fresh is this telemetry?"

Roberts glanced at his wristwatch. "I just got off the phone with Dr. Rohr about fifteen minutes ago."

Myers grunted.

"Master sergeant, did you run this by VLA, Arecibo, and Grand Bank?"

"Yes sir, I did. They were the ones who provided the asteroid's parameters to me and Dr. Rohr."

The lieutenant shook his head. "Damn fine analysis Mr. Roberts. I'm going to write up this crack analysis in your personnel jacket. Plan on a bonus."

"Thank you sir! But I have more news."

"What now?"

"The remaining fragments of the Gravitron asteroid seem to be reconstituting."

"Don't tell me they're a near-Earth threat too?"

"No sir. Not at this moment. If anything, this observed phenomenon will just be a footnote or a dissertation topic for some grad student.

"Thank God."

*　　*　　*

"Mr. President, we have another near-Earth threat."

"*What?* Dr. Shinto, I thought *Kamakazi One* destroyed it last month."

"Well Mr. President, Space Command reports that one of its six fragments is approaching our orbital plane. Dr. Paula Rohr, who first discovered this asteroid, is of the opinion that this rogue fragment, while much smaller than the original mother asteroid, is a planetary threat."

"Jesus! I just can't get a break … Who else knows about this?"

"You sir, me, Dr. Rohr, and Space Command. This data is less than a day old."

"Huh. So if this rogue hits us, what's the damage?" the president asked hopefully.

"Severe Mr. President. Dr. Rohr estimates a Torino 6 to 8 scale event."

"Which means?"

"Damage to the upper atmosphere due to a close flyby, to an impact creating severe local damage to the planet's surface."

"My God … and this is only a *fragment* you say."

"Yes Mr. President, just a fragment. If we do sustain an impact, the best case scenario would be a deep ocean impact that would result, depending upon where, damaging tsunamis."

"But if it hits land?"

"Severe local damage and considerable fallout. The

best analogy that I can offer you sir, is the explosion of the volcano Mount St. Helens back in 1980. Its debris cloud affected the planet's climate for over two years."

"What about a populated area?"

Dr. Shinto paused and then looked up with tearing eyes, "Worse than Hiroshima, Mr. President."

The president took a deep breath, and squinted at the ceiling of the Oval Office, "Thank you, Dr. Shinto. I have to get rolling on this. But before I do, I want you to immediately get in touch with your friend President Silver Moon. Coordinate with her on this. Give her everything you have on this fragment's telemetry. You never know."

"Consider it done sir."

*     *     *

As soon as Dr. Shinto left, the president reached for the phone and made a call to the Pentagon.

"General Cooks, I have an opportunity for you. Come on over to the White House for lunch."

The president noted a distinct pause on the other end of the line.

"What sort of opportunity Mr. President?"

"Ears only general. Trust me. You'll be glad you came. You'll love it."

\*   \*   \*

General Abraham George Cooks, the Air Force's representative on the Joint Chiefs, did not like surprises. On top of that, he bridled at being summoned like a servant by a president whom he considered a Washington neophyte. An immensely loyal and hard-working man, the call from the White House royally ticked him off as disrespectful. Still, he swallowed his pride, informed his personal secretary of his sudden change of plans to juggle his scheduled appointments, scooped up his hat, and made for the Pentagon's motor pool. During the walk to the garage Cooks took the opportunity to gather himself, and began to ponder about what the "opportunity" the president mentioned might be.

To the general's surprise, the president greeted him in the Rose Garden for an al fresco lunch, in a delightful, shady spot.

"General Cooks," the president began, "I wish this conversation to be just between us. A frank conversation. Far away from any prying eyes or ears. Can we do that?"

Sitting stiffly in his chair, the general's eyebrows rose, "Certainly, Mr. President."

"Good. Just one hour ago, I was informed that a

fragment of the Gravitron asteroid, Fragment Four, is a potential threat. Do you know about this?"

Flustered, the man replied, "Where did you get that intel from?"

"My science advisor, Dr. Georgia Shinto."

With a furrowed brow, "I see."

"General," the president said with a dismissive wave of his hand, "this information is barely an hour old, but I nonetheless wanted to share it with you so that we could jump on it."

"Yes sir. I understand."

The president paused as the White House's naval orderly placed two plates before them—open-faced cheese burgers with a side mound of fries.

After thanking the orderly, and then waiting for him to get out of earshot, the president continued. "General, I believe that you now have an opportunity to deploy your 'toy'," as he took a bite out of his burger.

Wiping off some errant mustard, the president went on, "If you leak what we are eating to my wife, I'll have to can you."

The general just continued to sit there, woodenly, with his hands in his lap.

"Not hungry, general?" the president asked mid-second bite.

"Yes, but . . ."

"But what?"

"Sir, the 'toy' as you put it, is not yet operational. It hasn't even progressed through its operational testing."

"You know general, I seem to be experiencing *déjà vu*. I seem to remember a similar conversation with nearly that exact reply."

The general didn't move a muscle.

"Here we are nearly two months later, and still the same answer." The president took his third bite and chewed it slowly, hoping for some sort of reply from his mute guest.

Cooks examined his hands, while his meal steadily cooled. His stomach rumbled. He considered his choice of options, but the president intruded on those thoughts.

"You know general, I well-recognize that this multi-generational project of the Air Force has cost billions to the American taxpayers." He pushed aside his partially eaten lunch, folded his hands before him, and leaned in. "I know general, because I looked. I also know that you inherited this project from your predecessors. So that makes this toy not yours, but the American people's."

The general's stiff face reddened.

"So, my most eloquent and talkative guest, where precisely is this toy of yours housed?"

"Wright-Patterson."

"You don't say. I want to see it."

"Sir, I don't—"

Now interrupting, "General, I said I want to see this toy of yours, tomorrow. Or are you afraid to share?"

\*   \*   \*

The pair stood at the entrance to a nondescript aircraft hangar located on the sprawling grounds of Wright-Patterson AFB. Yet, its importance was made obvious to the president just by the level of security that surrounded it.

"Mr. President," General Cooks began before they entered the structure, "you will be the first to see the *Omega* since President Reagan. To say that this is a highly classified asset would be a joke. The fact is sir, the *Omega* has no classification. It exists in a classification all its own."

After the double door entrance closed with an ominous click of multiple locks, they stood in darkness.

"Very theatrical general. Where are the lights?"

"One moment sir." The general began flipping

switches that ever so slowly powered up bank after bank of overhead mercury lamps. Their initial orange glow made the near-empty cavern look like Hades itself before they burned with a bright, white light. Unconsciously, the president shielded his eyes from their intensity.

"So general, what am I looking at?" the president asked about the black wedge that hovered before him like a cheap vaudeville trick. Despite the overhead lighting, its precise contours defied definition. Every photon seemed to disappear against its form.

"Over sixty years of development sir."

The president smiled full knowing this sandbagging general was still kicking, screaming, and holding back.

"So who's the toy's chief mechanic, cook and bottle washer?"

"Major Scott Shier, sir."

"I see, and where is he now?" the president asked as he ever so slowly began to circle around the floating, flat black, isosceles triangle, careful not to cross over the thick red line painted beneath it on the hanger's flooring. The words painted behind it said, DO NOT STEP.

"You know general, this toy of yours kinda looks

like a small Imperial Cruiser right out of *Star Wars*."

Cold silence.

The president abruptly stopped his partial walk around of the silently hovering craft.

"General, get Major Shier over here immediately."

"Yes sir." The general pulled out his phone and constructed a text, the length of which the president noted. He then viciously stabbed the SEND icon. No more than thirty seconds later, the president heard the general's device chime.

"He's on his way over Mr. President. Do you have any questions for me at this time?"

"Yes general, I do. Who initially authorized this project?"

"President Truman sir."

"I see. I didn't know that we had anti-grav technology back then." After a purposeful pause, "Huh. Then that makes this," pointing at the shadowy wedge with his thumb, "somebody else's technology. Would that be a fair assessment?"

"I cannot comment on that Mr. President."

"I kinda thought so." The president quipped as he continued his circuit of the craft.

Two-thirds of his way around the sound of opening locks and doors echoed in the cavernous space, followed by their closing and locking, and the approach of clicking heels. While the president watched out of the corner of his eye, he saw the general nod meaningfully to the major, who was dressed in casual Air Force blues—slacks and a short-sleeved shirt with an open collar. The man had folded and tucked his peaked cap under his belt. Lean and fit, he approached.

"Mr. President, I'm Major Scott Shier. I understand you wanted to see me sir."

"Indeed, major." Then turning, "That will be all, General Cooks. I would like some private face-time with the major."

Turning beet red, the general said evenly, "As you wish, Mr. President." He then stormed off toward the hanger exit, but not before pointedly eyeing the major once again. While the general departed, the president remained silent as he dug into his suit coat's pocket, retrieved his wallet, extracted a bright blue plastic card with a gold presidential seal, and waited for the sound of engaging locks.

He then looked into Major Shier's eyes. "Major, take a look at this card for a moment."

Examining the blue piece of plastic, the middle-aged man with hair cut high and tight frowned. "Is this the ID verification card for the 'nuclear football'?"

"Yes it is major," the president said while holding out his hand to get it back.

Placing it back in his wallet, the Commander-in-Chief followed up, "Can you imagine major, what the burden is like to be, of all things, a civilian granted with the authority to destroy the planet?"

"No sir."

"Well, major, I have been granted that authority by no less than the American people. Frankly, right now major, I'm interested in saving the planet. Can you respect that?"

"Absolutely sir."

"Now, before I ask you some questions, because I have a bunch of them, has anyone placed you under any sort of intimidation or coercion?"

The major looked down at his mirror-like black shoes.

"How long before retirement, major?"

"Three years, two months, and seventeen days, sir."

"I see. Where do you want to retire?"

"Montana sir."

"Like to hunt, fish?"

"You bet sir."

"Do you have immediate family?"

"Yes sir," the airman brightened, "A wife and two wonderful kids—a boy and girl."

"You are a lucky man major. Cherish them."

"Always do sir, every day."

"Now, major, I want you to think about your next answer . Where do your true loyalties lie? With the US Air Force or the defense of the American people?"

The answer to that question wasn't an obvious one. But the president was inwardly pleased the major stopped to consider his options carefully.

"The American people, sir," Major Shier answered with his chin high, vaguely defiant, and now standing somehow more erect.

"I'm pleased to hear that major, because I need to know if this *thing* here," again motioning with his thumb, "is capable of intercepting an asteroid that might be a threat to the Earth."

"Holy shit!" then catching himself, "Sir."

"My thoughts exactly major. So is *Omega* space-worthy?"

"Damn straight sir. It's been operational for some twenty-five years."

"You don't say."

"What precisely is your role regarding this … *thing*?"

"General maintenance, calibration, and flight prep, sir."

"So you're not a pilot?"

"No sir. To them I'm just a grease monkey."

Smiling, "I somehow doubt that self-deprecating characterization major, but can appreciate the gamesmanship that exists between airmen. So what's your official task designation?"

"Aircraft engineer, sir."

"Where did you study major?"

"MIT sir. I doubled in mechanical and electrical engineering."

"Very, very impressive major."

"*Thank you* sir." The major beamed with pride.

At this point the president turned to a sensitive issue and treaded carefully.

"Major, because of this conversation, what outcome do you fear the most?"

"The brig."

"*Really?* Anything else?"

"Dishonorable discharge and loss of my retirement."

"No kidding. Anything else?"

"A substantial demotion in rank and transfer to Elmendorf, Alaska."

"Yeah, I get that. I hear the black fly season there really sucks."

"And the mosquitoes can carry away small children," the major actually smiled.

The president sighed and shook his head. "Major, you talk to me straight, and I'll take care of you, your family, and will personally fund your retirement. You have my word. Deal?" he asked with an outstretched hand.

The major looked down at the proffered hand, and took it, firmly.

Thereafter, the president and major, now both on a first name basis, had a long and enlightening conversation as they walked around the vehicle, but not within the red line. But before he exited the hanger, and in front of Major Shier, the president made a personal call.

"Hey, it's me. Can you do me a big favor?

"No, not that.

"How do we immediately fire a member of the Joint Chiefs?

"No, not him, the Air Force guy, Cooks.

"Yeah.

"Uh-huh.

"Grounds? He flat out lied to me on several

occasions about our strategic capabilities. I can't trust the guy.

"Where? I'm out at Wright-Pat.

"Yeah, it's really something else to see.

"The press? Screw the press," he said as his free hand flew through the air.

"Just do it, like right now. And," winking over at Shier, "he's threatened one of our own."

"Yeah, I agree. Takes balls."

"Thanks buddy. I owe you one."

"Who were you talking to Mr. President?"

"The Secretary of Defense," he shrugged, "who else?"

"Holy shit! Just like that?"

"Just like that Scotty. I don't have time to screw around with memos. I have a world to save. Now not a word of this," the president said with an upraised finger. "Got it?"

"Crystal."

# CHAPTER 18

Stone woke up that morning fully expecting to begin his long journey back to the Old Oaks Academy, his students, lecture load, and his wife, Melaina.

"J.J.," President Silver Moon cheerfully greeted, "how's Egypt? I hope that I didn't wake you."

Glancing at his watch, Stone made a quick calculation.

"Just fine Betsy. It's eight in the morning here. That makes it one in the morning for you. So what's up night owl?"

"A change of plans. Your Egyptian sojourn has been extended. You're now officially on guard duty. It seems about a day ago a tracker sent an email with a set of highly sensitive coordinates to Barcelona. I guarantee the recipient of that email holds no love for you."

"This tracker, who were they?"

"A local Egyptian, but don't worry about him. The reverberations surrounding his death are abundantly clear. The Guardian claimed him."

"What do you have in mind Betsy? Were those coordinates of the gate?"

"Indeed. And given that the Vatican informed me of the situation, hang loose with their paranormal personnel. Fit in as unobtrusively as you can, and wait for something to happen. I well know that being reactive is not your preference. But for now at least, let's run with it. Ultimately, just between us, a side trip to Spain on your way home may be in the cards."

"Understood. Anything else?"

"Relax J.J., be a tourist, and enjoy the sights."

"Yes, Madam President."

\*    \*    \*

The evening before, Sister Busby gathered up Roth and Reissen for a similar discussion.

"It seems we have a breach," the dour nun began. "I have just been informed by Cardinal Alberti that the location of the 'monument'," she said indicating air quotes, "has been shared with a powerful member of the Hidden Folk. We, along with Stone, are now to remain in Memphis for the moment to quote, 'watch over things,' unquote."

Reissen's immediate reaction was positive. "This we can do. I will speak with Gretchen. We will just blend into the scene. I am quite sure that the pottery sorting tent could use our help."

"Good thought," Busby said. "But I want to first take a Hummer out and inspect the site, just to make sure."

"J.J. will want in on that excursion," Roth interjected.

"Ah, yes. I suppose you're right." Busby said. "It'll be just like old times, the four of us trundling around in the desert."

*   *   *

As the foursome neared the depression, Reissen once again had to stop the vehicle as he again experienced the heavy psychic weight emanating from the Gate of the Netherworld.

"J.J., the Guardian is frustrated, angry, and generally pissed off again." Pant. "Might I suggest you proceed most gingerly with your next conversation?"

"Thanks Erik, I'd be happy to. This is why they pay me the big bucks," Stone quipped. He left the vehicle, opened up the rear tailgate, and began donning his UCS. Moments later, the Lictor of Magic was nowhere to be seen.

Then his voice boomed over their radio, startling the trio. Turning down the volume, Busby said into the mic, "Take care out there, big guy."

"I intend to."

They once again followed Stone's progress in the sand, ghostly footprints that appeared out of nowhere.

Reissen shook his head, "I don't know how he does it."

"He's a professional Erik," Roth said. "He's battle-hardened. Best of all, he knows what he's doing."

\* \* \*

*Okay, First Soul, how should I proceed?* Stone whispered to his constant primordial companion.

***The old one is agitated. You said you would help protect the Gate. That is what vexes it. You gave your word. I would counsel an open, face-to-face meeting—unarmed.***

I must admit that last suggestion caused me to gulp as I neared the depression. Then, I clearly felt it stirring deep in the sand at my approach. As before, I went to one knee to psychically address something impossibly old.

*Oh great and might Kur, I failed to protect your Gate. I kneel before you—unarmed and ashamed.*

As I put aside my sword and 9mm automatic, I could literally feel the steady quavering vibration of its approach. The utter fear of holding my position against something so terrible and unknown approaching unseen, is hard to describe. One Halloween I peed myself when I entered my first haunted house. This, however, was on a far grander, more serious scale.

**You dare summon me *again* mortal!**

*Oh great and mighty Kur, I kneel before you ashamed at my failure to protect your Gate. I seek your understanding and forgiveness.*

**I grant neither. Only the Teacher of the Light Realm can grant such things. I am the Guardian of the Netherworld. I know *not* of such things.**

*Oh great and mighty Kur, then hear me out. It is in your best interest to do so.*

**You now dare threaten me?**

*No, no, oh great and mighty Kur ...* **Soul Carrier, allow me to speak on your behalf. Your words are clumsy.** The First Soul whispered to me.

***KUR! Do you know of me?***

**You are the First Soul of Creation, fashioned to keep the balance, and slay the wicked.**

*KUR! My soul carrier, this mortal one, this Lictor of Magic, means you no harm. But he does wish congress with you. Will you grant congress?*

**Freely, I will.**

And with that statement arose from the deep sands a great beast, beautiful, proud, and majestic in its own way. It stood three stories in the air, swaying side-to-side in agitation. It was a magnificent dragon, covered in jet-black scales, with ruddy red plumage along the crest of its head, spine, and tightly-folded wings. More bird-like than reptilian, Kur's canoe-shaped head and bill, easily twelve feet long, were filled with long, sharp teeth. Its huge round eyes glinted in the bright sunlight jade green. Its entire form shimmered in a bluish halo of static electricity that crackled and spat with each movement. The reek of ozone filled the air.

I couldn't help myself, "Damn, you're one handsome creature!"

At my compliment, Kur raised its head and coughed out a screeching cry in response. As its posture settled down, it began to preen its unfolding wings with its bill saying, **Mortal, disrobe so that I may see you.**

Stripping out of my UCS as quickly as I could, I answered, "Oh great and mighty Kur, I kneel before you to tell you that evil witches three desire to destroy your gate. I intend to stop them."

**This promised protection, which you have already sworn your word oath, has been for naught. But in deference to the First Soul which you carry, what do you propose?**

"Oh great and mighty Kur, I propose that we join together to stop these witches' threat. In so doing, your gate may suffer injury, but not destruction. As my bond, I offer my life." I said with my arms outstretched, the back of my neck exposed, defenseless, and vulnerable.

At this Kur's neck bent down low and snake-like as it eyed me in my submissive pose. It's nearing blue static charge made every hair on my body stand on end like a Van de Graaf device.

**Why should I believe you mortal ...** *this* **time?**

"Because if I do not stop the witches, and they indeed destroy your gate, then the Mortal Realm will be forfeit. That, I, and the First Soul, will not allow."

**So it is agreed. We have an understanding.** And with that, the long-necked dragon named Kur turned away, but not before brushing a pinion feather from its right wing against my left shoulder. The discharge of static electricity knocked me back several feet, stunning me utterly. **That was for not keeping your word oath,**

**mortal. Do not disappoint me again.** Then it slithered back into the deep sands and returned to its lair.

How did I know? I felt the absence of his emotional pressure, much like deflating a balloon. As for me, I struggled to sit up, my body numbed from the dragon's static discharge, my left shoulder now carried a bad burn where the feather made contact. Looking over at it, I knew it would surely scar magnificently.

I stiffly gathered up my UCS and weaponry, and staggered back to the Hummer in my shorts. Once there, I awkwardly got dressed, packed up my gear, slammed the tailgate close, and climbed into the backseat. Before Sister Busby could get a word in edgewise, I said, "Okay everybody, the coast is clear. Let's get on with checking out the monument's condition."

"But what about your shoulder?" Busby looked with concern.

"It can wait," I growled.

\*　　\*　　\*

Reissen, with deliberation, crept the vehicle forward and parked it next to the partially exposed monument.

"Looks like the wind has blown in a lot of sand," Busby remarked at seeing the state of the site. "Won't be long before it disappears entirely, yet again."

"I suspect that the Guardian has been slinging its fair share of sand around as well," Stone said.

The first thing that the archaeologist noted was the pristine state of the false entrance. "Look everyone! The three chips in the edging have disappeared. It almost looks like the monument repaired itself. J.J., have you ever heard of such a thing in your occult studies?" Reissen whispered.

"No Erik, I haven't. That's a new one for me." Stone sourly commented, "But that also explains the excellent condition of the inscription's glyphs." Then that significance finally dawned on the Texan. "And that sand-bagging S.O.B! It never once mentioned that the gate's construction was self-repairing." To which the First Soul drolly commented, *Soul Carrier, you never asked it.*

Then Busby did a very odd and techie thing, she began fiddling with her smart device. The usually frenetic nun then patiently waited with her eyes turned toward the heavens as if in prayer.

*Ring.*

*Ring.*

*Ring.*

Then the ringing died out altogether. It's battery finally depleted.

Turning around quickly, "There! Dig there!" Busby pointed. And in mere moments, the foursome, digging like dogs with their hands, had retrieved the source of the ringing—a Samsung smart device.

"Eww!" Roth exclaimed at finding the blood and sand encrusted device, which she then held between thumb and forefinger away from her.

"Let me see it," Sister Busby said.

"Yes, it's a mess for sure. Let's take it back to the Hummer and power this sucker up."

\* \* \*

While the retrieved device charged up, Busby began ticking off items on the fingers of her right hand. "Okay, what we found out today is the Guardian is one big honking dragon with awesome red feathers. Second, the gate itself is self-repairing, self-generating, *whatever*. Is that correct?"

Her three comrades nodded. "Stone. What was that lurid striptease in the sand all about?"

Stone shrugged, "The Guardian wanted to see me."

"What did you guarantee it this time?"

"My life."

"Huh. You don't say," the nun deadpanned.

"Lighten up Sister Josephine," Reissen said quietly. "The man did what he had to do."

The nun glared at the Austrian as if he had betrayed her. Then, she continued. "And finally, we have recovered what looks like the Egyptian tracker's smart device. Lord only knows what we might find on it."

# CHAPTER 19

The three witches of Barcelona decided to meet for dinner at a grimly appropriate place—the very restaurant where their coven had been butchered by the TIIIS Lictor of Magic. Their agenda was clear—how to unleash the Netherworld's inhabitants upon the Mortal Realm. From their point-of-view it was a grand enterprise, a giddy adventure, something commensurate and well within their collective talents.

"These coordinates, Portia," Marcia gushed, "How did you acquire them?"

A knowing smile, "I have my sources."

"I trust that your 'sources' are discrete," Julianna tersely added.

"More than discrete Julianna. They are dead, but enough about operational security, which I insist upon. I wish to entertain ideas on how to open the gate."

With her chin resting in her palm, Marcia dreamily said, "I am quite fond of what CMES Rome did during the Contest in the Aralkum Desert. That bomb drop was … breathtaking," she finished with a sigh.

"Marcia, a fine suggestion, but CMES Rome commands resources that we do not enjoy."

"We could ask them."

"Where have you been the last century and a half? Our coven severed its ties with Rome in 1870 remember? We were the 'wild ones' back then, too extreme even for Rome's pedantic tastes," Portia reminded. "Sisters, what we need is a plan, something that we can execute on our own."

"I have an idea," Julianna beamed. "Rent a tourist helicopter, co-opt the pilot while in flight, go for a ride over the desert, and drop a bomb atop the gateway."

Portia's eyes glazed over in deep thought at Julianna's suggestion. After several moments she returned to the here and now. "An excellent delivery system Julianna, what remains is the *kind* of explosive. Your idea implies something portable, the size of a large suitcase, and capable of detonating by a timer of some kind."

"Perhaps something nuclear?" Marcia drooled with eyes wild.

"Do you have access to such technology?" Portia snapped.

"No, but I am willing to poke around. What do you think the maximum weight should be?"

"Fifty kilos, no more, the less the better," Portia answered. "Remember, whatever it is, it has to be portable. Are there any other ideas? Alright then, Marcia, do your poking around. Julianna, look into securing in-country transport. As for me, I'll come up with a backup plan."

\*　　\*　　\*

With the smart device plugged in, it became clear a video had been in progress. Playing it back, the foursome saw first a slow pan of the monument followed by an extreme digital close-up of its inscription. Then a sudden blur of activity as the device fell face down, and came to rest against the sloped red granite face. Meanwhile, the device's audio input captured a grunt of pain and a shout in Arabic, clearly a choice expletive. Then heavy static slowly built up in the background, which transitioned into a raspy, grating sound.

Stone recognized it and broke the suspense, "That background sound you hear is sand in motion, or better, the Guardian moving through it."

*"Mein Gott!"* Reissen whispered.

The next twenty seconds of audio Busby turned down as the tracker's wretched screams were just too much to bear. When the recording came to an end, no one said a word. The silence of its finality was sufficient.

Sister Busby then searched around the device and uncharacteristically grunted out, "Shit. The bastard did send that email."

"What email?" Roth wanted to know.

"He sent an email with this location's coordinates to a Barcelona IP."

"Barcelona?" Stone asked.

"Yeah. J.J., you have some friends back there?" Sister Busby teased. "The best part is the Vatican already intercepted that transmission, but I now hold absolute proof of it, plus God only knows what else." The nun said while shaking the device in their faces. "Regardless, I got to get this to the techies back in Rome. They'll no doubt have a field day with it."

\*   \*   \*

Marcia Jordà already had a pretty good idea of where to start. Barcelona, after all, is a bustling Mediterranean city and port-of-call with a diverse population of over a million inhabitants. From her comfortable flat on the city's outskirts, the witch took the underground into the city. Destination—its core, the *Ciutat Vella*, or Old City.

Emerging from the subway tunnel and ascending the gray stone staircase, the delicious smells of a nearby pastry shop caused her to stop and make a quick purchase. Her sweet tooth's impulse satisfied, she began her rounds making subtle inquiries. Patient, pleasant, and methodical, the three hundred and nineteen-year-old witch hadn't made it this far by not being careful. Besides, her mentor, Portia, had drilled her on such things—often with harsh reproves at the slightest slip up.

In many ways, Marcia treated her quest much like one she conducted centuries before while searching for certain hard-to-get poisons or drugs like hellebore. At that time, she approached certain Greek merchants in the know, who secured for her the powerful Malian variety. In small doses her hellebore concoctions produced stunning hallucinations. Otherwise, it was a powerful and untraceable poison.

Now she sought a very *different* kind of poison—of the radioactive variety. Her targets were former Pakistani military officers, who while comfortably retired, always had valuable contacts for sale. She found them to be quite knowledgeable on a whole range of frightening subjects—but always for a price.

Four days later, Marcia had an appointment with just such a retiree, who currently was employed by an import-export firm. They met in his office located next to the city's dockyards. Instantly suspicious of the man's cigarette-stained atmosphere, Marcia reached out with her senses and found no less than four live recording devices. Before she took a seat before the man's gray industrial steel desk, she viciously fried them all with a subtle flick of her wrist.

Gamal Lodhra made the mistake of not rising when she entered his office. Smoking an unfiltered cigarette, he stubbed it out and gestured toward the open guest chair—also of hard gray steel. Next to it, she rested a brown leather executive briefcase.

"*Senyora*, what can I do for you?" the heavily tanned, gray-haired man with matching moustache asked in perfect Catalan. She sat modestly crossing her shapely legs, bare to the knee. His dark eyes, unashamed, scanned the attractive witch with open lust. Unconsciously, he licked his lips.

"*Senyor* Lodhra," Jordà pronounced with a silkiness not often heard, as her tongue seductively rolled the "R," "I require a man of genius and high intellect."

"Oh?" the man asked with slight quirk of a smile.

"Yes, *Senyor* Lodhra," again with the overemphasized "R," "I *need* a man who can move mountains." Her hands lay in her lap. Their fingers moved oddly. "Who will not stop at anything."

"I see, *senyora,* the man responded while slowly rolling his "Rs" in open imitation, proving to the witch the spell's affect. "What specifically do you *need*?" He leaned forward against his desk with an erection building in his slacks. A slight sheen of perspiration collected on his balding forehead.

"I understand that you were once an officer of some influence in your country's artillery force. I *need*," her fingers now becoming a blur of movement, "a tactical device, a W48, Mod-0 or Mod-1, to be exact. I also have recently learned that your nation has a considerable stockpile of these ... *discontinued* items."

Even with the external hormonal pressure that the witch employed, Lodhra remained stunned by the request.

"What you request, *senyora*, is quite substantial, requiring many transactions ... expensive transactions."

"I am not naïve to your *needs*, *Senyor* Lodhra," the witch purred. "In good faith, I will leave the one hundred thousand dollars US in this briefcase with you today. I fully understand your *need* to make arrangements. Further, I am most willing to *attend* to your *other* needs." She stood, rounded his desk, spun the man's chair, and knelt before him. When she placed her hands on Lodhra's inner thighs, the man experienced an organism like no other.

Eyes dilated, panting, and visibly flushed, the witch went to her purse and returned to bend over the helpless man. She slowly tucked her business card under his beltline. "*Senyor* Lohdra, when you have secured the merchandise, please call me, so that I can fully repay you for your troubles. I understand the current market price for such a device is eleven million US dollars. This I will deliver to you, personally, and in cash."

The entire transaction took seven minutes. After the woman left his office, Lodhra counted out the briefcase's contents—one hundred thousand US. He then greedily wondered how the woman would deliver the eleven million, already dreaming of the country estate it would buy. He smiled, already relishing their next meeting, for the woman had it all wrong. The going rate for the device in question was only *four* million US. Highly-motivated, he picked up his phone and called an old friend in the Pakistani Corp of Artillery at Nowshera.

\*   \*   \*

Incredible evil can reside in a compact space. Consider Pandora's Box. In this case, a hexagonal stamped steel shroud with tamper-proof tape, a numeric lock, and a logged lead inspection seal crimped into place, contained a true modern horror. The W48 Mod-0 artillery shell measured six and half inches in diameter by a little more than thirty-three inches in length. It weighed one hundred and eighteen pounds, and when detonated via an external conventional explosive, produced a yield of seventy-two tons of TNT—in other words, less than a kiloton of bang. It was every terrorists' dream.

Within the Nowshera armory, four special bunkers housed over two hundred and forty such highly deliverable and devastating instruments of death. The officer in charge of Bunker Twelve pulled one out of his inventory without batting an eye, on the pretext of inspecting its readiness for deployment. While on its way to the special weapons' inspection and maintenance facility, the nightmarish device went unaccounted for, proving what a bribe of ten thousand US could do. Soon afterwards, the misplaced item made its way off base in a loaded truck. In a nearby food processing plant, the device was transferred to a civilian vehicle, where it began an arduous overland journey of some seven hundred miles to the port of Karachi on the Arabian Sea. Once there, it found its way into a cargo container destined for Barcelona, Spain.

*  *  *

When Marcia next visited her retired Pakistani artillery contact, she came in an unmarked, white Mercedes panel van with two thick-necked thugs. In the back lay a shrink-wrapped palette of cash borrowed from the coven's vast financial resources. Initially, Portia had balked at the amount, but Marcia had insisted that she needed the bulky amount for show. Besides, she pointed out to her mentor, most of the US currency was out-of-date and therefore difficult to discreetly use.

Marcia also didn't think the bureaucrat would insist on counting it on the spot. She calculated that just one look of the palette's eleven million, would turn the greedy little man into mush. But just to make sure, she had brought along the two brothers for insurance, and to guarantee the consummation of the transaction. One could never be too careful.

Once again she sat demurely before the near-drooling Lodhra. This time, however, he did rise at her entrance and seated her. Returning to his desk, Marcia could see his nervous anticipation, his avarice, and the rank stink of his sweaty lust.

"Where is the device?" the witch asked, all business.

"In the warehouse below, where is my fee?"

"Also below, in a van in your parking lot. Perhaps we should conclude this transaction in your warehouse, out of the sight of prying eyes." The witch smiled.

"Why not here, now?" Lodhra almost begged.

"*Seynor* Lodhra," she said—again with those emphasized R's, "Have you ever seen eleven million US up close and personal?" She wickedly licked her lips with the tip of her pink tongue. Her right eyebrow twitched upward.

"No," gasp, "I have not."

"Then let's, together *senyor*, do so. The sheer smell of all that money alone is—so intoxicating."

They took the elevator down to the warehouse level, but Marcia stabbed a button to stop its course mid-floor. After several moments, it continued down.

When the elevator finally arrived, Lodhra's flush was telling, his normally precise tie akilter, and his belt partially undone. With a cracked voice, he ordered the smirking guard standing before the elevator to open the warehouse doors.

The witch then called the van's driver on her cell and instructed it to back in. The stark white Mercedes did so. When the warehouse doors closed, four heavily armed men quickly surrounded it.

"Do I detect treachery, *Senyor* Lodhra?" Marcia lightly asked.

"No, just extreme caution *senyora*."

The witch's two unarmed henchmen got out, eyed their competition, and dramatically opened the vehicle's two rear doors to reveal the plastic-wrapped palette. The bureaucrat gaped in disbelief.

"*Senyor* Lodhra," Marcia asked, bringing the man back to the here and now, "Does your warehouse have a forklift?"

With one snap of his fingers, one of the armed guards ran off. In the meantime, Lodhra fingers caressed the wrapping and said, "So this is what eleven million US looks like." Then, incredulously, he added, "Is it all here?"

Marcia, not at all surprised by the base level of the man's greed retorted, "Where is my device?"

"Oh, yes, that," as Lodhra nodded to another of the guards who left and soon returned with a loaded dolly weighed down with a hexagonal metal box.

Seeing the sealed box, "And how *Senyor* Lodhra, am I to open this?" the witch pointed.

Reaching into his coat, the man pulled out an envelope, opened it, removed a folded piece of paper, and tried to hand it to her. "Here is the combination."

"No, *senyor*. You open it. Here. Now." She commanded with force.

Shrugging his shoulders, he removed a wire cutter from his coat's pocket, snipped the seal, entered the code, and tore away the plastic security tape. The box opened like a hinged clam-shell. Within lay pure death. "Here *senyora*, at the blunt end is a small explosive charge. Its timer can be set for a maximum of five minutes. This switch with the safety pin starts the process. Just remove the pin, flip the switch, and the countdown begins."

Marcia smiled down at the weapon like a Cheshire cat with a bird in its mouth. She looked up to her men and nodded to them. With incredible speed, the pair disarmed and killed the three remaining guards, snapping their necks like pencils. She then grabbed the shocked Lodhra by the throat.

"And now you die, you pitiful worm. And just to be clear, my name is *Senyora* Jordà."

By the time the fourth guard returned with the warehouse's balky forklift, he found the warehouse's double doors wide open with four men dead on the floor. The device, woman, two men, and the white van were long gone.

# CHAPTER 20

Who knew that private helicopter tours in Egypt were so scarce, yet cab tours so popular? For a negotiated fee, a cabbie will take you nearly anywhere. For Julianna, she hired a driver with a late model Land Rover from the motor pool of her upscale Cairo hotel. Her pretext—she wanted to do some desert adventuring west of the Sakkaran Plateau.

After two dry runs that took the witch across the Western Desert to the Red and Black Pyramids, Julianna had her willing cabbie drive on to Alexandria and its harbor, where she picked up Marcia and her "delicate" cargo. Her colleague's choice of seagoing transportation had been a nondescript but luxurious Sicilian pleasure craft. Once Marcia's "luggage" had transferred to the Land Rover's spacious rear boot with their cabbie's help, they headed back toward Cairo.

While at their final gas stop where the cabbie replenished the thirsty vehicle's tank, Julianna placed a forgetfulness spell upon him and a thick wad of cash in his pocket. Deep down the witch knew this loose end should be gotten rid of, but she couldn't do it. She had taken a liking to the industrious young family man. Instead, she led him over to the gas station's refreshment bar, ordered a coffee for him, ruffled his curly black head, and abandoned him in a heavily stupored state. As for the Land Rover, she planned on abandoning it at the hotel's motor pool in the hopes that perhaps Ahmed would find it there. But for now, Julianna took over the controls of the vehicle, which she had memorized. Glancing over at Marcia, she grinned as she stomped the gas pedal. Next stop— Sakkara and their appointed destination.

"Julianna," Marcia chided once they were underway, "you have far too soft a heart."

"Perhaps, but now I can sleep tonight." Then, "Why don't you call Portia and let her know how we're doing."

"An excellent idea."

*   *   *

In all, it took the pair of witches nearly four hours before they reached the western fringe of the Sakkaran district. As it was, Marcia had successfully navigated them through a dizzying array of newly-built secondary roads that had connected countless desert communities.

Their plan was to avoid the congested traffic of the Nile Valley altogether, not to mention the security presence of the Egyptian police and military. Risking a stop and search of their vehicle would not do.

"So how does it work?" Julianna finally asked.

"Relatively simple: select any detonation time up to five minutes; pull a safety pin; flip a switch; and run."

"How far do we need to get before the blast?"

"Several kilometers at least, but the farther the better as far as I'm concerned," Marcia added.

"I'll gas us up before we drop it off."

"An excellent idea."

# CHAPTER 21

"My dear colleague, we have a big problem," Sister Busby said to the Austrian.

"What sort of problem?"

"Stone has been deployed to deal with a loose end in Barcelona. Meanwhile, the Vatican has just informed me that two of the Barcelona witches are currently en route to the gate. They are traveling overland in a vehicle. We have to get back to the gate before they do something extremely foolish."

"With what, sister? We only have two handguns."

"That should be sufficient." Now glancing about, the nun grabbed a handy table linen from the excavation's kitchen area.

"You get the Toyota, while I prep this cloth and grab two camelbacks."

\* \* \*

From the Memphis excavation at the Ptah Temple, Reissen drove like the wind. Even so, Sister Busby egged him on. As he neared the desert escarpment his sixth sense kicked in and a dire feeling of urgency took hold. When they arrived at the depression, his anxiety peaked to the point that he needed to urinate.

"Park atop the gate Eric," Sister Busby said.

Easily mounting the structure from an unexcavated side, Reissen skidded to a stop atop its smooth rooftop.

Getting out, Sister Josephina said, "Here, put this on," as she handed the archaeologist a full camelback. "I'm going to dig you in on this side of the gateway. Follow me."

Then conversationally, "Erik, are you familiar with how a sand viper ambushes its prey?"

"No."

"They bury themselves in the sand and wait, and that's precisely what we're going to do," the nun said while she dug out a long, low trench in the sand.

"Here, lay down. Get comfortable, settle yourself in, and don't move."

Reissen did as commanded as Sister Busby buried him up to his face.

"Are you claustrophobic?"

"No."

"Good," the nun said as she draped a portion of the thin table linen over his face and head.

"Can you see through the fabric?"

"Yes, quite well."

"Great. Now here's the plan. I am going to bury myself on the other side of the gateway opposite you. When the two witches arrive, we pop up out of the sand and kill them. Got that?"

"What's the signal to attack them?"

"Erik, that's for you to decide."

Then the nun covered his face with a light layer of sand, making sure that his eye sockets remained clear. Standing back several feet, Sister Busby regarded her handiwork with approval.

"Erik, you're invisible. Now don't even think of moving." And off she ran to get herself ready.

\*     \*     \*

Reissen soon found it difficult not to doze off in the sand's warm embrace. Childhood memories of idyllic vacations on Crete's southern beaches flooded his mind. With the camelback's hose inserted into the corner of his mouth, he had everything—including a loaded Vatican Glock in his right hand. When Sister Josephina ran off to take her position, the archaeologist was surprised at how the sound of her footsteps transmitted through the sand. In fact, he discovered that where he lay quite a bit was going on. More than once he was thankful for the linen covering his face. In one instance, a scurrying black scorpion passed right over his chest. Who knew?

A warm peacefulness slowly baked its way into the Austrian's consciousness. Not knowing the passage of time, he watched the movement of shadows, became mesmerized, and soon drifted off into a drug-like slumber. Annoyingly, a vibration woke him. Something was approaching. Then the sound of a motor's exhaust confirmed it.

*They're here.*

\*     \*     \*

The sight of the white Toyota Land Cruiser sitting atop the gateway caused the two witches to stop their hell bent progress in a long, sandy, sideways, downhill skid.

Squinting through the windshield Julianne said, "That truck looks abandoned. I don't see anyone. Do you?"

"The place certainly looks deserted. Drive up slowly and don't take any chances." Marcia said. "According to my GPS, that truck is sitting right atop our target. Drive up next to it. If all remains quiet, we'll unload, set the timer, and then follow those tracks over there to exit this little valley."

"Sounds good."

\*   \*   \*

Reissen watched through his sand camouflaged linen shroud as the white Land Rover cautiously inched its way forward from the Western Desert. Its passengers two women, were fixated on the Toyota truck. *Clever move*, the archaeologist realized. *Sister Josephina has quite a devious side to her that I would never have imagined.*

The Land Rover stopped right next to the Toyota atop the gateway. Its passengers nervously looked around, dismounted, and hurried to its rear hatch. There, they struggled to remove a heavy object, finally heaving and placing it directly upon the gateway's roof. One of them opened the metallic clamshell, performed some task, and closed it. Then, they hurried back to the Land Rover and prepared to leave.

*Wait a minute*, Reissen saw. *I recognize that box! It's a NATO artillery nuclear munition! I remember seeing them while I was on maneuvers in the Austrian military. How the hell did they get a hold of one?*

Before the archaeologist knew it, he emerged like a vengeful wraith from the sand, gun in hand, and running low toward the gate. He approached the Land Rover from its left blindside and closed in fast. Just as the Land Rover's engine ignited, Reissen began firing his Glock, first into the left rear tire, then into the left front. Both partially deflated tires caused the vehicle to sag on the driver's side, but not completely. Then the Austrian realized—*the tires are desert run flats!*

As the listing Land Rover accelerated, Reissen heard more gunfire, this time from directly opposite him. Sister Busby had joined the party, but unlike him, the nun wasn't firing at the tires. The archaeologist saw the passenger slump in a bloody mess, while the driver continued on transitioning from the top of the gate into the soft sand.

The Land Rover struggled, slowed, but fought its way stubbornly eastward out of the depression toward the Nile Valley. Its driver suddenly thrust her right arm towards her attacker, palm open, and fingers extended. A translucent ribbon of yellow light hit Sister Busby squarely in the chest. She reacted to the offensive magic as if she had run full tilt into a wall and collapsed. Seeing this, something snapped inside Reissen. He raked the driver's cab of the lumbering vehicle with withering fire, hitting the driver and decorating the inside of the windshield with gore. The Land Rover slowed to a stop in the soft sand. Its engine quietly idled, refusing to stall.

The Egyptologist had a choice to make. Go to his still Vatican colleague or attempt to save the gate. He chose the latter, sprinting back to the monument and the NATO munitions' container. En route, Reissen cooly revisited what he remembered about the weapon from his military days. One item stuck out—it would be no lightweight.

Huffing and puffing after having dashed back across the soft sand, the archaeologist mounted the structure and slid to a stop next to the metallic box, which refused to open.

"Locked!" he spat, *"Verdammt!"* Glancing around, the base of the nearby northern cliff caught his eye. "Move the thing over there," Reissen gasped out. "The Sumerian priest will understand."

Then and there the Vatican operative squatted down low and hefted the awkward one hundred and twenty pounds with his legs and back upright. He held it tight against his chest. He staggered, caught himself, and with deliberate purpose made for the cliff's base. It seemed like forever before he reached his goal. With muscles burning with exertion, he settled the canister amid the cliff face's rocky scree.

"RUN ERIK!" He unnecessarily shouted. Adrenalin-filled veins masked his overworked arm and leg muscles that sizzled with lactic acid. Lungs labored to supply much-needed air. Twice he fell. Twice he got up. In the end, he collapsed in the soft sand thirty yards beyond the gateway and next to Sister Josephina's fallen form.

"DIG!" he gasped. "And as for you sister, don't you dare die on me now!"

Chest wheezing, Reissen scooped out a narrow slit trench. It was nowhere near enough, but he grabbed the nun, pulled her in, and collapsed in utter exhaustion next to her. Only then did he make out her shallow breathing.

*Thank God. She's still alive.*

There, they huddled for what he dreaded, his mind overloaded with exhaustion and sheer terror. Reissen tightly pinched his eyes closed—waiting. Then, suddenly, the ground beneath them fell in.

\*   \*   \*

The device's explosive yield was rated at seventy-two tons of TNT. However, for a variety of technical reasons, most due to poor maintenance and the improper placement of the conventional explosive trigger, the detonation fizzled. Nonetheless, this fizzle created a massive crater that displaced untold metric tons of rock and sand upon the gate, burying it utterly, but practically speaking, leaving it untouched. The heat generated glazed the crater's interior and sent a towering mushroom cloud of debris into the blue sky. The blast's concussion was felt eight miles away at the Dhashur military base. At first, many frankly thought it was an earthquake. The detonation's yield amounted to only two tons of TNT, only 2.08 percent of the weapon's design.

*   *   *

The two Vatican agents slid down a good thirty feet into a sandy cavity, where they came to rest within a circle of large black scales, sheltered by a huge wing of red feathers. In the darkness, a basketball-sized jade eye stared at them through its nictitating membrane.

"Kur," Reissen whispered to the eye.

**Indeed. It is I.**

Then the earth moved. The air was sucked from their lungs. Reflexively, the archaeologist opened his mouth and his ears popped painfully. The concussion shook him to his core, threatening to rearrange his internal organs. Reissen lost consciousness.

After an unknown amount of time, Reissen slowly came to and blinked away the dust, sand, and grit from his eyes. Disoriented, the archaeologist blurted out into the darkness of the space, "What just happened?"

**An attack on my Gate. It failed because of your uncommon bravery.**

"Huh?"

**I perceive that the event has addled you. I will return you two to the surface when all is settled. For now brave one, sleep. Your destiny was not to die here, for you have far too much ahead of you. Now brave warrior, forget.**

\* \* \*

As luck would have it, Flight Lieutenant Mustafa El Mahdy was the one in the air minutes after the airfield's siren went off. With all of the excited chatter in his headphones, he didn't need to be told where he was going. The menacing plume to the north was obvious to all on base. Flipping open his flight log strapped to his right leg, the pilot scanned his personal notes—the ones about the missing two men in the desert and the mysterious rectangle buried in the sand.

*What's up with that area?* He groused to himself.

Now airborne and rapidly closing in on the mini

mushroom cloud, his base commander warned unnecessarily over the tactical radio, "El Mahdy, stay upwind of that cloud. We don't know if it's radioactive."

"Understood."

"Also, El Mahdy, report anything odd."

"Understood. Out."

With the cloud dead ahead and drifting south toward the Dhashur airbase, all the ground personnel went into scramble mode, donning emergency gear and masks. Meanwhile El Mahdy flew due west and away from the drift path, while his co-pilot, Pilot Officer Hamid Galhouley, manned the video camera and recorded everything.

"Sir, what do you think happened?"

"Unknown. That's why we're in the air. But it sure doesn't look good."

El Mahdy righted the helicopter's northerly course three kilometers out in the Western Desert. From there, he could easily see the profile of the plume as it lazily floated away from its source, leaving behind a thinning tendril that reached to the ground.

"Galhouley, we're going to loiter out here for the some minutes to allow that cloud to dissipate over the target. Then we'll do a fly by. Be sure to get some good video on the first pass. I'm not eager to fry my nuts a second time."

"Understood."

Even so, El Mahdy cheated. He flew his rotary aircraft past the blast site several hundred meters to the north of its still wispy crater. Yellowish-white blast rays of calcined limestone extended out in all directions. What had been once a sandy depression nestled between two steep-sided cliffs, now was leveled. The crater had taken out the northern cliff and its concussive blast had collapsed its neighboring southern ridge. Nowhere could the rectangle be seen as it was buried. The shattered remains of a vehicle littered the eastern perimeter. But remarkably, the two pilots gasped in total disbelief as a figure waved up at them from below. Next to him lay another, who appeared injured.

"By Allah's gray beard!" Galhouley blurted out.

"Command, this is Rover One."

"Come in Rover One."

"Command, there are two survivors on the scene. Please advise."

"Rover One, what do your instruments say?"

"Hovering between two to three Rads at two hundred meters."

"Rover One, this is Air Commander Gabril Provide assistance at your discretion. Do not land if your instruments read fifty RADS or more. Over."

Galhouley looked over to El Mahdy with a pained look. The flight lieutenant answered his co-pilot's silent plea to flee by descending and voicing a sharp order. "You heard the Air Director. Monitor that instrument! We're going to do this by the numbers."

# CHAPTER 22

The sixty-four dollar question was—how do you kill a cagey veteran witch of over one thousand years, who is also a member of the Hidden Folk? My smartass answer—very carefully. But seriously, how does one go about such an ambitious task? Instinctively I understood the challenge in layers, where several scenarios could be followed or shifted to depending upon conditions. But in order to figure out those situations, I looked to the collective wisdom of my witchy wife Melaina Makris and a good colleague, Mr. Dexter. Between the two of them, this Texan figured he would have couple of sure-kill ideas.

"So, where do you intend to confront this witch?" Mr. Dexter wanted to know from behind his Louis XIVth office desk.

"Probably in her Barcelona flat."

"No, Lictor of Magic, that is your last choice," Mr. Dexter sourly said, "That is absolutely your last and most deadly choice for a confrontation. You never, ever, confront a witch on her home turf. Instead, you need to get her on neutral ground, somewhere out in the open, and as far away from her domicile as possible."

My wife nodded in agreement with wide-eyed emphasis.

"Okay, so noted." I back peddled. "I admit that was a bone-headed idea. So how do I somehow draw her out?"

"J.J., how do you want to kill her?" my wife bluntly asked, her face all business.

*God I love her!*

"Swiftly. Any confrontation in a public venue would require it."

"Agreed," Mr. Dexter confirmed. "Do you intend to use your sword?"

"Yes, but if the situation requires, I'll use my suppressed hand gun." Stone said. "I don't think lethal magic will be effective, not with her."

"Indeed, I agree lethal magic will be useless against her. But simple hand weapons will require you to get close," Mr. Dexter emphasized. "I seriously doubt she will allow that."

"Why?"

"Your sword and hand gun have already proved their effectiveness upon her kind. She knows this. Your near-approach will be surely detected."

"How?"

"Your aura, Lictor of Magic. It sticks out like a sore thumb in any crowd. Your pretty bright platinum glow is rather distinctive."

"Can it be masked?" I hopefully asked.

"Ah, in your case, that would be some trick."

"How so?"

"Since every soul possesses an aura, not having one would be immediately obvious to her."

"What about me?" Melaina interjected into this two-sided conversation.

"You?" Stone asked with surprise.

"Yes. Why not? You, you big lovable oaf, would make a marvelous distraction."

"Ah, *la femme fatale* … now that would be delicious," The Frenchman said into his steepled fingers. "That she would not expect. The killing stroke, however, must be quick and brutally sure. *Non, Madam* Melaina, I envision you in a supporting role, not as the killer, but rather the one who makes sure of the kill. Regardless, *Monsieur* Stone, your mind must remain blocked as to what *Madam* Melaina is up to. Without question, this assassination will be dangerous, potentially injurious, and maybe, if one of you is clumsy, fatal."

\*   \*   \*

It was a gloriously brilliant Barcelona morning. Seagulls pivoted and soared on the thermals of a powder blue Mediterranean sky. Not a cloud could be seen. Portia Le Fey sat on her balcony festooned with fragrant red and yellow flowers. It was her morning ritual, to greet the early sun, and her private time to sip her creamy Vietnamese coffee. The witch found it amusing to gaze down into the cathedral's square at the garishly dressed tourists, who faithfully followed their guide's bright yellow flag like so many mindless sheep. With their incessant camera clicking, Portia mused about how infinitesimal the capacities of their short and long term memories must be. *So this is what they think a vacation is. How do they even find the time to review their images?*

She turned her head away, utterly dismissing the churning crowds below. *The start of such a fine day,* she decided. *Little do they know how their lives are about to change.* The ancient witch imperiously preened as she again looked down through the thick wrought iron railing. Images of succulent cattle ran through her mind. She then smiled. *Marcia's call from Egypt had been so marvelously encouraging. Those women have come so far so fast.* The thought swelled her chest with pride. *I taught them well.* Then, after several moments of consideration, *Odd, I haven't heard from them since. Perhaps I should give them a call.*

\*   \*   \*

Meanwhile, Melaina sat in the cathedral's square thoroughly enjoying a concoction of her own design. Before her, still untouched, waited a breakfast tapas of smoked salmon on toast garnished with fresh dill, lemon juice, and capers. Her huge papyrus sun hat hid her Alexandrian face from the already glaring morning sun. Her blocked mind shielded her from the powerful sensitive's perception overhead. Occasionally, the Alexandrian witch peeked up from beneath her sunhat's broad brim at her target—Portia Le Fey. Her address had been thoughtfully supplied to TIIIS by the Vatican.

*The woman seems to be doting over her clutch.* But that disapproving thought was banished by the tiny earpiece in her left ear.

"Sitrep?" her husband, J.J. Stone, asked.

"She's on her balcony drinking coffee, and gazing about taking in the plaza's tourists. From your vantage, she should be in plain sight," Melaina said softly into the mic hidden in her bright teal sundress made of Egyptian cotton.

"Yeah, she is. Perfect," Stone said.

\*    \*    \*

This particular morning, Portia's glorious mood took a sudden turn, when she felt a decided ripple in her highly tuned perception. The sensation best reminded her of a bow wave from a speed boat running full out across a mirror-like lake.

*Well, this is an interesting development*, the witch thought as she automatically went on high alert. Coffee cup still in hand, she first scanned the square below and sensed nothing amiss. Confused, her delicate Dresden cup suddenly exploded in her right hand as a composite silver-lead bullet passed through it, managing during its flight to ruin her left ear lobe. Blood spewed. A shocking wave of pain immediately engulfed her, shattering her idyllic repose.

*Use your newly acquired precognition!* Portia chastised herself. Unfortunately, her darkly augmented temporal sense failed her. She saw nothing; smelled nothing. As there was no sound of a gunshot to home in on that only added to her distress.

Stone had laid in wait upon the sun-kissed red tile roof of a five-story building two hundred and seventy-three yards away from Portia's balcony. That was what his range finder had told him. The light bending cloaking effect of his armorer's NSE material had rendered him and his rifle practically invisible. To any passersby, who might chance to look up, they simply were not there. With the sun over his right shoulder, his low profile threw little if any shadow across the tiles. His position on the roof's forward slope also guaranteed no shadow silhouetted against the blue skyline. The subtle cough of his heavily suppressed weapon defied recognition from the streets below.

Portia, momentarily frozen in place, and still not sensing any threat in the immediate neighborhood, clenched her teeth in frustration. Being a helpless target was not her cup of tea. Portia prided herself as a woman of action and aggression, as a hunter and not the hunted. But in this instance, her plight had gone unnoticed as blood from her ruined lobe flowed down her collar bone, ruining a white silk blouse.

The arrival of the second sniper round, however, did snap Portia out of her initial confused shock as it burrowed its way into her left shoulder. At impact, she yelped, spun, and fell from her chair. The second silver-lead slug seared and fragmented inside her. The round's custom grooving reacted as designed.

Now sprawled across her balcony, Portia gritted

her teeth, while her mind screamed. *Do something you idiot! You're being poisoned!*

The witch finally did the obvious and cast a disappearance spell as she lay profusely bleeding on her balcony's decking. Once so shrouded, slowly, she made as best she could for the doorway, which she had left partially open. Before she moved very far, the witch thought, *I cannot see my attacker, but can I feel them.*

She stretched out her right hand and viciously closed it. Her finely manicured fingernails bit deeply into her palm. Blood flowed. Portia whispered a handful of words, and then smiled, *Ah, there you are, you son-of-a-bitch! Now I have you!*

\* \* \*

"Two hits. She's down, but surely not for the count. I can no longer see her," Melaina softly said into her mic.

"Yeah, I saw them too. Get in position." Stone whispered back from his rooftop position two blocks away. "I've lost her as well. That means she's cast some sort of camouflaging spell. I'll tell you when." Eye still fused to the eyepiece of his rifle's scope, Stone lowered his field of view to the bottom third of the partially opened balcony doorway—her only means of escape, and waited.

Then a blinding pain hit him, as if a massive vise had been applied to the sides of his head, squeezing. Blood began to flow from his nose and ears. Stone's vision blurred, then he heard his internal partner warn him, *Fire again, soul carrier, several times! That monster has found your blocked mind!*

Fighting through the agony and bloody tears that threatened his aim, Stone's Marine training took over. The rifle coughed twice in quick succession, bracketing a point where he thought his target might be ...

*     *     *

With agonizing slowness, Portia crawled her way toward the doorway on her right side, while her right hand held Stone's mind in a death-squeeze. Mimicking a side stroke, she could feel the telling effects of blood loss and the spread of systemic silver poisoning. As she struggled on, she fought slipping out of consciousness. Her left ear numb and useless, she knew all too well that her brain would be next. When she reached the doorway, she carelessly pushed it open all the way.

*     *     *

In position since before dawn, his patience had paid off with his first two rounds. His target now lost, he had to wait again, but now his head wanted to explode. Somehow the witch had found him. He dared not move an inch out of fear of rolling off the high roof. His equilibrium shot, all he wanted to do was puke. Then, sudden relief, as the psychic pressure released following his two last rounds. But still Stone didn't move. The post-stress reaction felt like his body wanted to float away. Then the nausea hit. Green, seasick, and unsure of himself in such a precarious position, he shook his head to clear it. Sucking it up, he peered again through his rifle scope just as witch's balcony door swing inward, he paused two beats, and vertically bracketed two more rounds across the lower third of the opening, guessing at his quarry's camouflaged position.

\*　　\*　　\*

Once again mind-numbing and excruciating pain jacked through Portia as two more silver-lead slugs dug their way into her lower back and right shoulder blade. Her right hand went limp. The crushing psychic spell on Stone failed.

With her life's blood freely flowing, the woman now realized her legs couldn't move. Her spinal column had been severed during that last fusillade. Her legs were useless. The witch's only chance was to make it to her conjuring room. Once there, she could recuperate rapidly and then deal with her unknown assailant.

*No*, Portia thought bitterly through the agony, *only one mortal would dare attack her so openly—that damn TIIIS Lictor of Magic! He's already claimed so many from my coven!* There and then she vowed she would not go so quietly into that good night.

*   *   *

Following their plan, Melaina ascended the five sets of stairs to the landing of Portia's flat. In her left hand she carried a white plastic grocery bag filled with several items. In her right, the Alexandrian wore her mother's silver rings of power. She removed from the bag a pair of awkward wooden-soled sandals and put them on. Nervously, she stood before the threshold of the Barcelona witch's wooden door. The Egyptian witch held out an open palm of her right hand toward it. Melaina felt a distinctive buzz in her right ear and a hot tingling from the tips of her extended hand.

*Powerful magical defenses reside here!*

*   *   *

Stone watched through his rifle scope as a much-bloodied and struggling witch flickered back into view.

254

*Her injuries have broken her concentration on the camouflaging spell.*

As he watched, the witch lay still. The smeared trail widened beneath her, forming a pool. Then he saw it. Her left index finger was moving, writing something in that precious liquid upon the wooden flooring.

*Soul carrier!* The First Soul screamed into his consciousness. *Finish her! Finish now!*

Stone reacted instantly, firing the last three consecrated silver-lead rounds from his rifle's clip. The first two he saw as impacts along the upper spine. The third walked into the back of the witch's head. From his vantage point, a red mist resulted that looked like an exploding watermelon. The witch's left finger went limp. The writing stopped.

*Why?* He thought.

*Because she was preparing a death wish spell you soft-hearted imbecile! I have lost two soul carriers to that desperate tactic! The only good witch is a dead one.* The First Soul concluded.

*Even Melaina?*

No return comment came from his internal tenant.

Stone grunted into his stalk mic. "Subject down … presumed dead. Move in … with extreme caution," he told his wife.

"Understood," Melaina replied from outside the witch' flat.

Only then did Stone begin a slow, cramped crawl backwards over the roof tiles. As he did, he too left a blood-streaked trail. A fact that was not lost on him.

\*　　\*　　\*

Melaina took a pair of white cotton gardening gloves from her plastic bag and slipped them on. Next, with eyes closed in genuine reverence, the Alexandrian prayed in greeting to the apartment's defenses in her mother's long-dead magical language. Then, focusing specifically upon the door's lock, she prayed again. It clicked open. With a gentle push from her right hand's pinky finger, it swung open wide and inviting, while she spooled up a powerful defensive spell.

The sharp, heavy smell of copper and death wafted forth. A gruesome looking form lay within. Melaina took a thick cylinder of kosher salt from her plastic bag, opened it, and heavily sprinkled the door's threshold before crossing over it. She repeated this ritual as she slowly entered deeper and deeper into the flat, crunching her way as her wooden soles encountered the thick crystalline grains. Melaina approached the ruined body, raining down a steady coating of salt, avoiding all contact with Portia's bloody pool, which had engulfed her right hand and the writing on the floor—canceling it utterly.

When the salt ran out, Melaina opened another from her bag, and continued the salty snowfall now directly upon the spilled blood and corpse. The effect was quite telling as the blessed salt came into contact with the fallen member of the Hidden Folk. Wherever it came into contact with the already shrunken and ash-gray skin, tiny craters of saline formed. A similar phenomenon occurred with the fallen one's blood, as the dissolving salt purified it. When the second cylinder went empty, Melaina produced a third and final one, and now generously covered the body as if preparing it for roasting. Finished, the corpse had already collapsed in upon itself by a good third.

Now carefully retreating from the flat, crunching her way upon the insulation of blessed salt and neutral wood, she carefully closed the flat's door with her right pinky finger. When its lock clicked closed, she shuffled away, scraping away the shoe's embedded salt crystals in the hallway's carpeting in the process. By the time Melaina reached the ground floor, she removed her special shoes and replaced them with sneakers. A few yards away, she discarded the white plastic bag and all of its contents in a trash bin.

\*    \*    \*

The Devourer of Souls smiled at the newly silver-injured arrival as the drool of anticipation dripped from its hideous maw. "I have been waiting some time for this delicious moment."

But the dark soul of Portia Le Fey didn't cower. "I'll just bet you have, you lying, two-faced, son-of-a-bitch! Your supposed powers of precognition didn't help a damn against that Lictor of Magic! In fact ..."

The Devourer had heard sufficient from this ungrateful wretch as it promptly tore the floundering soul asunder, more to silence its screeching than to satisfy any hunger.

\*    \*    \*

The morning of Le Fey's death, the hunter contentedly sat in the courtyard below sunning itself. Hiding behind a pair of mirrored Ray Ban Aviators, its eyes flicked this way and that. The hunter wore its straight black hair in a thick braid that protected the back of its neck. Undetected by the preening Elder of the Hidden Folk above, it causally inventoried the many passing tourists, always on the lookout for an opportunity. Dressed in stylishly torn jeans and a faded AC/DC concert t-shirt, the hunter blended in and looked just like its prey.

Every aspect of this day's hunt changed, however, the instant the Elder fell injured. Its acutely sensitive ears heard a series of strange coughing sounds, tasted the air, and scented fresh blood, which caused its mouth to water. While its hearing sensed the direction of the attack, it had difficulty locating the source in the bright morning sunlight.

*Somewhere over there, and above*, it judged.

For some reason, the movement of a woman in a large sunhat and billowing blue sundress caught the hunter's keen eye. It turned its head fractionally. She carried a white plastic shopping bag. But there was something about the woman, something special, that marked her as worthy of observation. So it did.

Unlike the rest of the humans, who appeared oblivious to what had just taken place above their very heads, this woman seemed to know and moved with purpose. As proof, the woman in blue casually strolled off in the general direction of the fallen Elder's flat and eventually entered its arched portico. Seeing this, the hunter bestirred itself, and moved to another position to watch and see what might happen.

After seven minutes, the woman in blue reappeared

from the flat's portico, again walking with purpose. Oddly, she deposited the white plastic bag, its contents, and her sunhat into the nearest trash bin. Her now free flowing black hair blew in the breeze as she hurried away down the street.

Now more than curious, the hunter went over, retrieved the bag, and inspected its contents. What it found was telling—three empty cylinders of blessed salt, and a pair of wooden-soled sandals—marred with flecks of blood and embedded grains of salt.

*She is the accomplice to the Elder's murder. The salt sterilized the scene and prevented any chance of the Hidden One's revival. The wooden-soled sandals prove that she is an adept, if not a witch. They would have insulated her from any passive defensive magic of the Elder's flat.*

The hunter returned the bag to the barrel and retrieved the discarded sunhat. Holding it close to its nose, the hunter breathed deeply, fully scenting the woman's perfume down to her shampoo. One item stuck out—the heady smell of the lotus blossom. *She's probably Egyptian*, the hunter concluded. *That would match her appearance quite well.*

Returning the sunhat to the bin, the hunter breathed in the air as it walked in the direction taken by the woman in blue. As it followed her trail, the hunter's mind churned.

*She looks Egyptian, smells Egyptian, and even wears the lucky blue color of an Egyptian. She's Egyptian. How interesting ...*

Arriving at the next intersection, the hunter looked around and in the distance saw the woman in blue waiting at the curbside. Fearlessly it continued on and closed within twenty meters of its quarry. Then, a plain, white paneled van stopped. Its gaping side door opened, and the woman in blue disappeared within. As the vehicle pulled away, the hunter memorized its license plate number.

*Interesting. This was a well-planned murder from start to finish.*

\*   \*   \*

Later that day, Portia's cleaning lady Maria, inserted her charmed house key into the old witch's door lock Upon opening the door, the ripe and sickeningly sweet smell of death struck her like slap in the face. Then upon seeing the grotesquely desiccated corpse of her long-time employer stretched out on the floor, Maria let out a wail of shock and horror that alerted the entire floor. Minutes later, the police arrived.

# CHAPTER 23

The Barcelona homicide detective let out a deep sigh. As he reread the coroner's report his cigarette trembled between his nicotine-stained fingers. He squeezed out a final puff before he stabbed the singed filter into his desk's overflowing ashtray. Sitting back under the stagnant smoke, his mind churned and formulated, making him think dangerous things, taking him to places he didn't want any part of. Born and raised a Roman Catholic, none of what he was considering could be sanctioned by the Church. But the case before him was, nonetheless, clearly something far beyond the Church.

Without doubt, after his thirty-two years of service and three failed marriages, what he now contemplated was the stuff of fiction—paranormal fiction. That old television show, *The X-Files*, came to mind. Then again, he reminded himself that a homicide was a homicide. He had his victim. What he needed was a killer and a motive. That was where things got even stranger.

Returning to the forensics file also on his desk, its contents really muddied the waters, especially those two pages about the victim's "ritual room," and the multiple samples of dried human blood taken from it—only some of which matched the victim. And then there was all of that salt ... a macabre pattern was beginning to form in the detective's mind.

Victor Mañas rubbed at his gray two-day old stubble in a vain attempt to clear his mind. It hadn't worked. If anything, the action told him to reapply himself to the case. Above all, Mañas needed to talk to someone, so he called up the coroner, Dr. Marti Valles, and arranged for a private meeting.

The pair agreed to meet at a nearby pastry and coffee shop. This was to be a serious discussion—one that required sugar and caffeine instead of alcohol. As the hour was mid-afternoon, the shop was deserted; its divine aromas still lingered. After the pair made their "cholesterol-free" choices, they sat down. From across the room, the pair looked like brothers.

"Marti, thank you for agreeing to meet me here. I am deeply concerned about a recent homicide. I want to talk about it."

"You mean the one with the decomposed mummy?"

"*Sì*, that one. I have been checking my files. It is not the first such case. There was the massacre in the San Martí district, where sixty-two victims all ended up pretty much the same. Remember that one?"

"How could I not, I and two others had been assigned to it. That one was gruesome. Are you saying that these two cases are connected?"

At that point all conversation stopped as their waiter appeared with their coffees.

"No, just the victims' postmortem state of preservation—or lack thereof, is very similar."

"Well Victor, I think there is more here than meets the eye. In both cases, silver played a significant role."

"Precisely Marti. What is the percentage of people who are allergic to silver?"

"Low, if not infinitesimal. In fact, skin allergies due to silver jewelry are rare and take decades to manifest. Nowhere in the medical literature have I ever seen any reference to festering, ulcerated sores, or the like surrounding a wound. Yet, in both of these cases, I observed just that in sixty-three examples. Victor, have you ever asked yourself, 'who were these people?'"

"Yes, I have."

"And?"

"I have only heard rumors, Marti. Unfortunately, in

homicide, we work with rumors a lot. Some call them tips. But a strange thing happened after that massacre some two and a half years ago. Barcelona's homicide rate dropped by nearly sixty percent."

"That much?"

"*Si*, and rather suddenly, the odd murders suddenly stopped."

"Such as?"

"Exsanguinations, missing body parts, ritualistic murder and dissection, torture, outright predation ..."

"Oh, come on, Victor."

"Marti, tell me, for instance, how can a traffic victim lose both of his livers? There are three cases of that scenario alone, which to me, smacks of someone trying to cover up a far more serious crime."

The look on Marti's face remained skeptical.

"I think it's high time you checked your department's files more closely," the detective chided.

Now back peddling, "Come to think of it, Victor you may be right. Business has been slow. But what you're saying is the massacre of those sixty-two was somehow beneficial?"

Victor shrugged and leaned in. "Now Marti, here is what I have heard on the streets. That massacre was of a coven, a very notorious one that was considered so out-of-line that a hit team was called in."

"A coven of black witches?"

"And perhaps *others*," Victor said without batting an eye.

"What *others*?"

"That, my friend, I do not yet know." With open hands almost pleading, "Again, I am only dealing with rumors straight out of folklore and myth—the stuff of children's nightmares. But I ask you—how would you characterize the remains found at the recent homicide?"

Now it was Marti's turn to shrug. "Other than the extremely atypical decomposition of the subject," the coroner said, "the subject was gunned down by no less than eight bullets—many of them fragmented—I believe purposefully. A ninth round was found imbedded in the wooden flooring of the apartment, proving that the murderer fired from above, probably a rooftop. That said, the slugs were made of a curious amalgam of the purest silver and lead—an interesting combination that suggests expert knowledge of ballistics, bullet manufacture, and armament. Get this— the slugs were sniper rounds with boat-tailed ends to improve their flight stability. Their tips had been grooved to fragment on impact. Since they were an amalgam of silver *and* lead, a highly specialized gun barrel was not required, since silver is harder than lead. The wounds caused by the silver ingredient reacted very poorly with the victim, becoming grossly festered almost gangrenous. I can only conclude that the victim's constitution must have been highly allergic to it. In short, whoever did this, really knew what they were doing and were prepared to do it. And, somehow, they knew that the victim was highly allergic to silver."

"So silver poisoning for all sixty-three," Victor stated.

Another noncommittal shrug. "Looks like it."

"Marti, how old do you think that woman really was?"

"We know she was dead for maybe five hours tops. Her maid's discovery proves that. As for her decomposition, mummification, whatever you want to call it, that suggests she was dead far longer."

"How 'far longer'?"

Pinned into the corner, the medical coroner rubbed his chin and balked at answering the question directly. "Victor, have you ever seen an Egyptian mummy?"

"Sure."

"Maybe that old."

*"Mare dolça de Déu!"* the detective whispered.

The pair paused to address their sweets and

coffees. After several minutes of thoughtful silence, the coroner asked the homicide detective, "So Victor, who is doing all this killing?

"I haven't a clue. The rumors make no sense. I just get great sighs of relief at the mention of the coven's passing."

"But a few minutes ago you mentioned a 'hit squad,' your words. Where did you get that notion?"

Victor examined his empty plate, his fingers drumming. "Only in passing. Several sources assumed it was, given the butchering of the sixty-two with a sword."

"*A* sword? That suggests a lone killer, not a squad of them. Victor, what are you suggesting here?"

The detective deadpanned, "I think we might have a very special vigilante roaming our streets."

Silence.

"Victor. What can kill sixty-three black witches?"

"I sincerely do not know, Marti." With a lame smile, "Perhaps a hit squad of witches?"

"Do you think this is the work of the Vatican?"

"I certainly hope not."

The detective paused to sip his lukewarm coffee. He grimaced.

"And then Marti, we got this anonymous tip. It was

posted mere minutes after the murder. Someone saw a woman leave the victim's flat, deposit a grocery bag and sunhat in a garbage bin, and leave in an unmarked, white panel van. They even provided us with its license plate number."

"You're kidding."

"No, I am not. It was an airport rental. We're in the process of tracing down who rented it. Your department is processing the contents of that bag and the sunhat right now. Maybe we will be able to lift some fingerprints and DNA."

"We are close Victor. But DNA is hard to nail down."

"Marti, there's another twist to all of this."

"Yeah, what?"

"The victim's smart device. For the past several days she's been in constant contact with two others in Egypt. The authorities there haven't been able to locate them. Their hotel reports that their rooms haven't been touched. And one email contained a video of an ancient monument, complete with the GPS coordinates of it."

"Okay. So where are you going with this?"

A shake of the head, "Here's the best part Marti, a massive explosion was reported at those coordinates."

"How big is 'massive?'"

"Don't know. The Egyptians didn't say. But it was something big enough to register on their seismometers."

\*   \*   \*

Unlike the city's homicide department, the fall of the Barcelona coven did not sit well with the hunter. The sheer act of the grand massacre and balcony assassination shocked it. This creature, while rudely shunned by the Hidden Folk, stalked the region in quiet anonymity. Its relations with the Barcelona coven, while grudgingly acknowledged, had always been conducted at arm's length. As a consequence, it never appeared on any roll or document; never appeared in any tale. In many ways, this it preferred, this obscurity, as it frankly required little in the way of social contact. To do so might threaten its preferred taste for human prey. However, when the last of the coven was destroyed—the venerable Elder Portia Le Fey, it became angry. She had been the only one who had shown it any respect. Besides, in many ways, the well-known excesses of the coven had provided ready cover for its predation.

Born the spawn of a vampire father and an Iron Age human, this particularly long-lived dhampirica was marked with straight black hair, a prominent Roman nose, and large dark eyes. Some found her "look" at best artistically intriguing, at worse the gaunt shade of a concentration camp inmate. A diet of human livers staved off aging, heightened the woman's five senses beyond human levels, preserved its finely textured skin, and if allowed to gorge, built muscle mass. Oddly, she threw no shadow and hunted vampires for sport. This last was the principle reason why the Hidden Folk had rejected all her overtures for membership, as many within its ranks were in fact her prey. Her name was Dannica, "morning star," in Danish.

# CHAPTER 24

For Reissen and Sister Josephina, their return to Rome was a blur, following their pickup by the Egyptian helicopter and its crew. After the detonation, their absence from the Memphis excavation caused Roth, Wald, Peters, Franks, and its director quite a bit of concern until they were informed that the two were safely en route to Rome.

Once back, the nun was admitted into the Vatican infirmary with a severe concussion, damaged ear drums, and a heavily-bruised sternum—the legacy of a full-on offensive magical bolt of energy. The Austrian, however, had gotten off far easier with only a minor concussion.

"So tell me, Dr. Reissen. What happened out there?" Cardinal Alberti began his debrief with a mixture of concerned anxiety and suppressed anger that one of his own had been injured.

"A white Land Rover arrived at the site from the Western Desert with two women and a NATO-grade nuclear munition. Once they armed it atop the monument, they attempted to flee. Sister Busby and I stopped them. She killed one and I the other, but not before Sister Busby was struck down by a flaring bolt of magic. I removed the canister from the monument and set it aside the northern cliffs. Then I returned to my colleague, dug a trench, and together we rode out the blast. The next thing I knew, an Egyptian helicopter was overhead, which picked us up."

The cardinal, who had been sitting back deeply in his office chair, noted with considerable interest that Reissen was not blocking his mind, but he still had possessed the discipline to keep his energetic psychic bubble in check. Then he pointedly asked, "Is that all that occurred?"

"All that I can remember, Your Eminence."

"What, utter, nonsense," the cardinal slowly said. "Do you really expect me to believe that the two of you survived that blast in an open trench and at that range?" Shaking his head in negation, he answered his own question. "Not on your life. Dr. Reissen, what are you holding back?"

"Your Eminence, I am holding back nothing. The last memories I have were waiting for the blast, needing to relieve myself, and then feeling the wash of the helicopter's presence overhead."

"I see. Do you mind if I try something rather unorthodox?"

The Austrian shrugged, "Not at all."

"Now, Dr. Reissen, sit back into your chair, close your eyes, and relax deeply." The cardinal soothed as his fingers flew in odd patterns. "That's it. Relax."

The cardinal gently probed the Austrian's mind, trying not to pry beyond his short-term memory. What he found amazed him. While the cardinal's journey is difficult to describe, an analogy would be looking for an address in a strange city. Looking here and there, and following the street signs and their address numbers, Alberti finally arrived at a desolate plot of land. With not one shred of construction or weed, the section was raked flat and smooth, down to its perfectly manicured rows of soil. Still and all, traces of memory lingered on the wind, which suggested some details of what had happened to his charges.

What seemed like only moments later, Reissen awoke relaxed and refreshed. "How did I do? Did you find anything?"

Guardedly, the cardinal answered, "Dr. Reissen, you and Sister Busby experienced the blast while underground. That is all I could resurrect from your memories."

"Underground?"

"Yes. It appears that some agency sheltered the two of you underground. Then, once the blast cleared, you were deposited on the surface. What do you make of that, professor?"

"I do not know, Your Eminence. I am very confused."

"Indeed, you rightly should be. There is the taint of magic surrounding your memories of that blast. This residue is very ancient, if not primordial. Do you still have nothing to add?"

Searching his mind, the Austrian found himself at a loss. "No, Your Eminence. I have nothing."

"How unfortunate. It is not often in a man's life that he brushes up against something truly that ancient."

The cardinal looked down at his desk top, shuffled several papers, folded his hands before him, and continued.

"Dr. Reissen, you have performed admirably for Pro Deo. In many respects, this first deployment was a test of your training and innate abilities. On all counts, you have exceeded my expectations. My question for you is, do you wish to remain a member of Pro Deo, or return to your university career in Vienna?"

Reissen, uncharacteristically, took his time in

responding, something that the cardinal noted.

Finally, "Your Eminence, I wish to remain. However, if I do, I request an office in which to work and a flat."

The cardinal grunted, "Done, on both items. Your office will be located here, within the Gregorian Museum. Space is tight, but as you already know, our library is quite ample. As for your flat, I have arranged for one with furnishings. As before, the parking of your car is your affair."

Again the cardinal fingered the pages before him.

"Dr. Reissen, our records show that you are unmarried. Is that correct?"

"Yes, Your Eminence."

"Have you ever considered joining the clergy?"

Again Reissen paused before answering.

"No, Your Eminence. I prefer my social freedom. I chafed while in the Austrian military. Joining the clergy I imagine would be much the same. So, no, Your Eminence, at this time I will pass on that offer."

The cardinal nodded once in acknowledgement.

"Well then, Dr. Reissen, allow me to be the first to formally welcome you to the ranks of Pro Deo. Be prepared to continue your training in the various ... arts, as they are sometimes called. By the way, Sister

Gabriella wishes a word with you."

Reissen left the cardinal's office moments later and retrieved from Marta, his secretary, two slips of paper and a key, which required his signature. The key was to his new office along with directions to it. The other piece of paper was the Rome address of his new flat. Glancing at it, the Austrian judged it to be within easy walking distance from the Vatican. These he stuffed into his pocket as he made his way to Sister Gabriella's office.

In the past, Reissen's previous visits to the old nun's office caused him a certain amount of anxiety. But this time, the Egyptologist was more curious than anything else.

As was his habit, the archaeologist locked down his mind well before arriving and found the nun's door open and inviting. He knocked on the wooden door frame to alert its occupant.

"*Entrare*, Herr Professor Dr. Reissen!" Sister Gabriella beckoned from behind her desk.

Reissen, surprised by her use of his full and formal academic title, then saw the diminutive nun round her desk to greet him warmly.

"Erik!" she said taking his hands in hers, "I am so very happy to see you in one piece! Sister Busby has told me all about your adventures. Please take a seat."

Once again ensconced behind her overloaded desk, the ancient nun began, "I wish to thank you for saving Sister Busby's life. What the two of you did out there in the Egyptian desert was far beyond admirable. But what *you* did, impresses me greatly."

Reissen allowed the nun's words to wash over him like warm surf.

"Thank you, Sister Gabriella. I did what I had to do."

"Indeed, you did," the nun said with a slight smile. "Just so you understand, Erik, we are few in number. The loss of just *one* can be staggering to our cause."

\*     \*     \*

Half a world away Melaina Makris and her husband J.J. Stone were undergoing a similar debriefing. They sat before Stone's laptop in Myers Hall on the Old Oaks campus. His office made for a cramped but cozy environment.

"So, you two, how did it go?" President Silver Moon leaned in close to the screen from her office in Santa Fe, New Mexico.

"The witch Portia Le Fey is dead," Stone pronounced. "I shot her eight times with composite silver-lead rounds from a nearby rooftop. Melaina confirmed the kill and sterilized the body and immediate area."

"So many shots?" the president asked. "Isn't that a bit of overkill?"

"She was a tough old bird," Stone deadpanned. "Besides, she was in the process of casting a death wish in her own blood."

"Huh. Have either of you heard about what happened in Egypt?"

"Only in outline," Melaina said. "Our pilots said something about a big blast and that Drs. Busby and Reissen somehow managed to survive it."

Now it was President Silver Moon's turn to shake her head. "Hang onto your seats. While you two were deployed to Barcelona, the two other Barcelona witches attempted to nuke the gate of the Netherworld. They failed due to the efforts of Drs. Busby and Reissen. We can only suspect why or how. But the good news is that the gate is now safe and sound buried under tons of rock and sand."

"How did Drs. Busby and Reissen survive that?" Stone wanted to know.

"That's the sixty-four dollar question. From what I have been told, their entire survival story was magically wiped from their minds—the operative words being 'by very ancient magic.'"

Makris and Stone sat back straight at that tidbit. "By the Gate Keeper?" Stone surmised.

Silver Moon shrugged and said, "That would be my logical assumption."

"Curiouser and curiouser," Stone remarked quoting Alice's famous line from Louis Carroll's *Alice in Wonderland*. "It seems that the primordial's have their secrets too."

"So it would seem," Silver Moon mused. "The result is that the gate has been hidden once again. The notorious Barcelona coven is finally finished, as the charred remains of two women were found at the blast site."

"By the way," Silver Moon asked, "is there any possibility that either of you were seen in Barcelona?"

At this point during the debrief, Stone and his wife looked at each other, frowned in thought, and shook their heads in negation. "I don't think so," the Texan said.

# CHAPTER 25

Somewhere out there, history was in the making. Over a 384 bit encrypted channel, a brief conversation took place between the "ground" and its "charge."

"PITSTOP, this is SKIPPING STONE. Capture net has been successfully deployed. Over."

"SKIPPING STONE. We have you all on radar five by five," The Houston native said. "Go easy boy and good hunting!"

"Roger, PITSTOP. Over," Mission Command Jeremy Cassell said into his stalk mic as he worked the control paddles of the external control arms, which moved like the arms of a Praying Mantis. When fully deployed, Cassell fanned out between the appendages netting made of a special nanoweave of carbon-fiber and artificial spider silk. His actions were similar to that of a Brazilian net fisherman. The only thing missing was the weight held tight between his teeth.

Cassell had to chuckle about the guy from ground control. "He's probably one of those rabid NASCAR fans."

"So how are you doing over there, Jerry?" Mission Pilot John William Griffith, wanted to know.

"Pretty good. No tangles. Should have this ensnared soon. There's not a smooth surface anywhere to be seen. The real trick will be disengaging the net when we're finished. I really don't want to jettison it."

Fifty tense seconds later, Cassell had sweat stains on his tightly fitting mission head sock that completely covered his dark curly hair. It, and the form-fitting body suit, protected him and his partner from the magnetic field of their craft. This was accomplished by tethering their suits to the vehicle's ground with a cable. Then, finally he declared, "Bingo, Johnny boy! We've caught us one big fish!"

In reality, the commander had snagged the asteroid by one of Fragment Four's jagged outcrops. The scene was ludicrous in the extreme, like a minnow latching on to a fin of a full-grown northern pike. Still and all, an attachment was just that.

"Way to go, Jerry. Commencing low gee ferrying operations, initiating at ten centimeters per second, on my mark … Mark!"

Moments later Cassell thought he heard a slight groan from craft's fuselage, but dismissed it as his imagination.

Meanwhile, Griffith ever so slowly applied pressure on the snagged net. "Accelerating to fifty centimeters per second. How's your net doing Jerry?"

"The grappling net is stable and holding," Jerry said to the nervous Griffith.

For the next fifty minutes, this well-seasoned team of two slowly and gradually pulled Fragment Four out of and away from the Earth's orbital plane. This first ever space ferrying operation took place at a distance of approximately one AU—the distance from the Sun to the Earth. Before that, for the last month the administration had them collecting large and sometimes dangerous orbital space debris. Interspersed between their main garbage duty, they latched onto other stuff like nuts, bolts, solar panel fragments, the odd work glove, and the ever so popular ten and seven millimeter sockets lost during repair excursions. While maddening, as there were more than four hundred thousand bits out there to clean up, but Jerry and Johnny understood what it was for—valuable maneuvering practice for potential planetary emergencies just like this one.

"Ferry operation complete." Johnny said, "Time to cut it loose."

"I'm on it. Give me a minute or so to tease the net free."

Moments later, "Yo, Jerry?"

"Yeah."

"What do you think that hunk of rock is worth?"

"Plenty. Radar says that it's mostly an iron-nickel asteroid. But guess what, I'll bet my lucky quarter that it contains lots of silver, gold, and platinum too."

"You don't say."

"Plus really scarce rare-earth minerals that are far more valuable," Cassell added.

"You're not going all geologist on me, are you?"

"Nope. Just trying to stay current with our new mission plan."

"You know it's a damn shame that we can't bring this puppy home," the pilot added.

"I hear you brother. But just wait. Once Washington decides to go public on this sweet technology, asteroid space mining will be a reality, and then the stock market will go absolutely bananas."

"You got that right."

And with that said, Jerry reeled in his precious netting and retracted the manipulation arms back into the craft. That task completed, he sealed the long ventral bay doors—a design feature that was later pirated by the designers of the NASA Space Shuttle Program.

\*    \*    \*

A newly-minted Colonel Scott Shier monitored the SKIPPING STONE's ferry mission from the ground command bunker at Wright-Patterson with a mixture of fatherly pride and sheer awe. Once conceived as the ultimate strategic weapon, the *Omega* now towed certain death and destruction away from his home world, potentially saving billions of lives. *So this is what it feels like to make a real difference ... Boy do I like it!*

# CHAPTER 26

Ley lines have always been curious entities. Made of pure psychic energy, their paths crisscross the globe in a fixed and complex network, while each exhibited the characteristic vagaries and emotional mood swings of bio-chemical individuals. Depending upon the ley line, contact might, at first glance appear fickle, as some show pure indifference for the human condition, while others manifest a broad range of mischievousness to outright hurtfulness. Still others are known for their benign assistance.

Their well-documented and charted variability in temperament has led some psychic experts to speculate upon their origin. Some argued for a primordial gestation during the formation of the planet, in essence making the ley lines the original inhabitants of the planet. Other sensitives, however, saw in the ley lines the ultimate origin of mankind's many regional mythologies, with the ley lines portraying the many "personalities" reflected in the gods and goddesses of a particular human culture.

The classic example quoted by this school of thought is the Achaean Ley Line, which manifested through the Oracle of Delphi, a barefoot, psychic priestess in a chthonic setting, usually an underground grotto. Its influence was understood by the ancients as possession by the god Apollo, who provided a client's questions with prophecies and answers in dactylic hexameter.

Without question, the initiation of psychic contact between a ley line and a human sensitive was a delicate matter, much like the dangerous courtship rite between spiders and praying mantis. Rejection is common and can be sometimes fatal. But once such a bonding is consummated, it is for life, to the benefit of both parties.

*     *     *

High in the Swedish Kjølen Mountains, south of the towns of Grong and northeast of Snasa, the first telekinetic pair prepared themselves for their ordeal. Bleak, treeless, and windswept, with jagged rocks covered with yellow and light green lichens, four hearty individuals huddled together wrapped in arctic parkas. As a prudent precaution, they had left the warmth of their Land Rover some one hundred meters below and behind a ridge. They even disconnected its battery cables.

Drawn by lot, these two telekinetic sensitives had the honor to be the first to offer resistance to the fast-approaching asteroid fragment. Guided by their remote-viewing colleague, these two were to join with the Strömkarlen Ley Line, well-known for its helpfulness and approachability.

Jenna Olhaufsen was one of these heroes, a middle-aged sensitive from Oslo and member of TIIIS. Ruddy-skinned, full-cheeked, and with deep laugh lines tickled by errant wisps of graying blond hair, the smiling woman seemed completely at home atop the peak. The other hero, Safir Gasar, of Palestinian birthright, was one of the six CMES volunteers. His deep olive complexion seemed to dull to gray in the wind and low temperature. With his face wrapped in a scarf, he was all brown, expressive eyes with long black lashes. He gently bobbed, while sitting cross-legged on a cleared patch of the rocky surface, in a vain attempt to generate some heat.

This pair's psychic guidance mechanism was a plain-looking woman. Sitting with her back to the wind, Marta Gonzalez, a Spaniard and member of TIIIS, looked like a human-sized Eskimo igloo devoid of detail. Her normally ebullient demeanor remained hidden in the biting cold.

The fourth member of this psychic spearhead, Mr. Henri Dexter, didn't have to be there at all, but had insisted as he was the one who had devised this psychic defense grid. With sixteen pairs strung out like a string of pearls that extended from Sweden to The Devil's Tower in the Black Hills of the United States, Mr. Dexter wanted to be on the scene to directly take command if necessary. This master wizard of offensive and defensive magic had a trick up his sleeve and if things went poorly, was more than willing to use it.

"My dear colleagues," Mr. Dexter spoke through his muffler, "it is time to dig your bare toes into the lichen. Gently reach out to the Strömkarlen. Make your introductions. Explain with your thoughts the vital nature of your intrusion upon its solitude. You have forty-five minutes to accomplish this crucial task."

As the three did so, Mr. Dexter unnecessarily scanned the skies above, but only saw fair blue heavens and fluffy white clouds. Not normally a religious man, the wizened Frenchman nonetheless silently recited a prayer from his youth. Oddly, the pious act granted him a modicum of peace.

At thirty-seven minutes into the exercise, Gonzalez

hoarsely announced, "I see the asteroid. When you are ready, each take one of my hands and I will guide you to it."

Two minutes later, both Olhaufsen and Gasar confirmed their linkage with the ley line far below the mountain range. Old hands at such things, both recognized the familiar tingling electricity in their exposed toes that they sat upon. While pleasurable at first, both knew as the psychic power mounted, their extremities would amp up and twitch.

"Thirty seconds to commence," Mr. Dexter quietly said. "And, may God watch over you all."

As the Frenchman began his countdown from ten, Jenna and Safir removed their heavy gloves and joined hands to balance out their telekinetic pulses. Both breathed deeply and rhythmically in preparation.

"NOW!" Mr. Dexter shouted.

Both of the telekinetic athletes began their assault on the celestial object with grunts of effort. Their tightly held hands seemed to throb between them. A bluish fog formed around them, reminiscent of static electricity, but rather was a byproduct of the psychic plasma that they pulsed up and into the sky. Both Gonzalez and Dexter moved away from the phenomenon. What had begun as a pulsing stream of energy much like a machine gun's tracer rounds, quickly intensified into a continuous beam that slowly traversed across a section of the heavens.

"How are they doing?" Mr. Dexter asked the remote-viewer.

"They're squarely on target. In fact, they are digging a furrow along the asteroid's center section."

"Can they break up the object?"

"Not a chance. It's too big," Gonzalez said sadly.

Under the enormous strain of conducting the ley line's power, Jenna's face reddened. Her generous cheeks ballooned in and out as she hyperventilated. Sahir's eyes pinched together while his nose freely bled, leaving a growing dark spot on his white and black checked scarf.

Three minutes and forty-three seconds into their shared ordeal, Olhaufsen whispered in her mind to her joined colleague, *Can you feel it?*

*Yes! It's like trying to push a broken down truck. At first, no movement. Then, slowly, it moves.*

*Yes! Sahir we're doing it!*

*Indeed ... Jenna ... we are.*

At that moment of elation, the sensitives surged their efforts ... briefly. Mr. Dexter and Marta Gonzalez clearly witnessed this change as the once bluish fog that surrounded the pair turned into a blinding, brilliant white. And then, suddenly, it blinked out, leaving them with after-spots in their eyes.

"Quickly," Mr. Dexter called to Gonzalez, "help me with them!"

Both sensitives were lying on their sides facing each other, spent, apparently unconscious, but still holding hands.

*   *   *

Jenna giggled as she wriggled her pudgy toes in the warm surf. "I've never been in the Mediterranean before." The pear-shaped adolescent said in her favorite, faded, blue one-piece swimming suit.

"It's fun, Jenna," answered back the gangly boy, all arms and legs, with unruly black hair, a broad grin, in baggy red shorts.

Now with a serious face, "Sahir, you haven't had that much fun, have you," the young girl asked.

"No, I haven't," Sahir, the boy said, while looking down at the sand. One hand absently fingered it.

"You're such a good soul Sahir, you should try to have more of it," the young Jenna said with a touch to his bare shoulder. "You deserve it. You're a hero, Sahir."

"I am?"

"Sure, we both are. We moved that asteroid."

"Yeah, we did, didn't we?" The boy brightened. His grin had returned like a morning sunrise.

\* \* \*

"Tilt his head back, while I plug his nose with some gauze. We have to staunch this bleeding," Mr. Dexter said to Gonzalez.

While the Spaniard carefully propped up the Palestinian's neck in a make-shift pillow of hats and gloves, she quietly said to the Frenchman, "They moved the asteroid."

"They did!"

"Yes, quite a bit." Now looking up into the Frenchman's eyes, "Mr. Dexter, your plan's a success!"

\* \* \*

Across the globe in the asteroid fragment's shadow, thirty-six telekinetic sensitives reveled in relief and joy when their remote-viewers confirmed that they had accomplished what many had considered the impossible. But something more had taken place. Each pairing of once strangers were no more. Instead, something quite unexpected resulted. The channeling of the ley line's power had bonded each to one another.

President Silver Moon shook her head in utter amazement at the coordinated feat as she keyed in the good news along with a profound message of thanksgiving into her laptop. When the Navajo stabbed the SEND icon, three individuals received her e-mail: Mr. Dexter, who had marshaled Project Damocles; Chairman William DeSalvo of CMES, who had generously volunteered his best; and her good friend, Dr. Georgia Shinto, the National Science Advisor to the president, who had so audaciously considered asking TIIIS for its assistance in the first place.

\*   \*   \*

Colonel Scott Shier, still bathing in the afterglow of victory, caught the eye of a lieutenant who was waving him over to his station within the command bunker at Wright-Patterson.

"Sir, I think that you should see this."

"What am I looking at lieutenant?"

"This is an acceleration graphic of Fragment Four sir."

"Okay, I can buy that, but what's the problem?"

"Sir, this line here, this gradually rising line, represents what the *Omega* did to the asteroid's deflection from the orbital plane."

"But what about all those spikes?" Shier wanted to know.

"That's the problem, sir. Those spikes represent sixteen accelerations that I cannot account for."

"What do you mean, lieutenant?"

"Sir, we had some serious help from *somewhere*."

# CHAPTER 27

Victor Mañas ran the reported license plate number that the anonymous tip provided. To his surprise, the van was not stolen, but a hire, rented from an agency at the Barcelona-El Prat International airport. Armed with a name and a bank credit card number, Mañas followed a trail through a dizzying data maze of security authorizations and protocols.

At first he ignored the name as he suspected it to be an alias. It was the credit card's number that he focused on. Slowly a coherent picture began to form around a corporate entity with branches located throughout the world, with a US address for its headquarters. Its name was odd—The International Interface and Integration Society.

A sigh of relief blew through the detective's lips. *It isn't the Vatican. But who are they? What's their motivation for murdering an elderly woman?*

After several minutes of research, the homicide detective sat back in his chair, his head filled with disbelief. *Deu Meu! They're a paranormal research organization!* He stopped to rub his tired eyes as his head filled with the spooky forensic details of silver poisoning, blessed salt, accelerated decomposition, and a mummified corpse.

Next, just to make sure he was not going crazy, he opened a private file from his desk's side drawer. It contained notes of his interviews about a dark coven rumored to be about seventy members strong. Again he sat back. *Sixty-two massacred two and a half years ago, and now, another, plus the two in Egypt. It looks like someone is trying to wipe out an entire coven.*

While the detective routinely dealt with organized crime and the local gangs, was it such a fantastic leap of faith to imagine something similar in this case? *But why? What was the motive? What did that old woman do that deserved this?*

What Mañas now struggled with was the obvious and beneficial effect of the sixty-five's permanent removal. His city's murder rate had plummeted. The odd and grisly had petered out. Then came another thought. *Should I even pursue this? I can think of several departmental colleagues who would rejoice about such a result.*

Again he rubbed at his face, hoping to awaken himself from this conflicted nightmare, when another thought hit him squarely between the eyes. *What was the motivation of the anonymous informant in the first place? Is he or she one of the last remaining members of this coven, perhaps fearing for their life? Was their call a desperate plea for help?*

Momentarily fixed on that thought, Mañas, just for the sake of completeness, typed in the name on the bank credit card and hit his computer's ENTER key. Nothing was retrieved from the local database. Shifting gears, he tried again, this time on the Interpol's database—again with no success.

Then he remembered the informant's precise description of the woman dressed in blue and took a chance. Ignoring all the domestic flights within the EU since the credit card appeared to be US-based, the detective searched the US-bound flights and found two on the day of the murder. Next, he accessed the airport's security video archive, and settled in for a long session.

To Mañas' amazement, after only six minutes of searching he found his suspect. Checking the customs and immigration video, he again found her, but now had a name—Dr. Melaina Makris, her passport— Egyptian, and a flight to the US aboard a corporate jet. No surprise, the Gulf Stream V carried a North

American serial number on its tail. After some further sleuthing, he discovered the jet was owned by TIIIS as well. This revelation elicited a grunt of satisfaction from the homicide detective. Feeling lucky, he next contacted the Egyptian authorities. They confirmed the woman's passport as valid, and additionally supplied some background details, which were not much help.

The trail ended there. A US-based paranormal organization appeared to be involved in the murder of an old woman. That was all Mañas had. He had no fingerprints, no DNA from the discarded sunhat, and crucially, no motive. But then there was the back story about a dark and brutal coven out-of-control and a plummeting murder rate. As intriguing as it was, he still could not move forward. He had nothing to sell to his superiors except circumstantial evidence—the details of which he could not share out of fear of ridicule or worse. Frustrated, Mañas decided to take a vacation.

*     *     *

As soon as Inspector Mañas initiated his query about Melaina Makris on the Interpol database, the Vatican knew about it. For as part of the informal treaty between the Holy City and TIIIS, was the exchange of personnel information precisely for a time like this.

With the inspector's searches henceforth red-flagged by Vatican security, Mañas' passport information request to the Egyptian authorities, Pro Deo knew about as well. In fact after both of those contacts, the Vatican's security division spiked the inspector's computer, and while he slept, copied his hard drive and Cloud storage. By the time Mañas woke up the next day, the Vatican knew everything that the inspector knew about the murder of Portia Le Fey.

At this point, Cardinal Alberti, the operational head of Pro Deo, was ordered by his superior to contact Inspector Victor Mañas personally. This the cardinal did, in person, the next day.

The cardinal sat uncomfortably beneath a thick layer of cigarette smoke in Mañas' departmental office. The cleric wore plain clothes, dark slacks, a dark sport jacket, and an open collared white shirt. The man sitting before him behind the desk clearly needed a shave, and by the look of his nicotine sweat-stained shirt, a shower.

"Thank you for stopping by, Your Eminence. Visit Barcelona often?" Mañas opened as he lit another. At the action, Alberti unconsciously winced.

"Inspector Mañas, I visit Barcelona seldom by choice," the cardinal coolly began. "There are, or perhaps I should say, *were* elements within your city's population that Holy Mother Church did not approve of."

Mañas grunted, "You're kidding."

"No inspector, I am not. I am told you have been recently struggling with a particularly vexing homicide. I am here because I have been instructed to answer any questions that you might have regarding it, in order to put this matter ... aside."

Now squinting, "Your Eminence, are you trying to bribe me?"

"Not at all inspector. All I offer is information given freely. All you have to do is listen ..." shrug "... or not."

Mañas listened ... for two hours. After the cardinal left, vowing openly to burn his clothes, the homicide detective looked over in the mirror above his personal sink.

"Damn. Where did all that gray hair come from?"

\* \* \*

Unknown to Makris and Stone, they had indeed been seen in Barcelona. Or perhaps better—detected and stalked. The entity which had done this, was not happy about the murder of its friend Portia Le Fey, far from it.

In fact, and before the police arrived, it had viewed the ruined corpse in her flat. The heat of anger and the overpowering desire for vengeance flowed through its veins like molten metal. For the first time in a long time, the hunter named Dannica contemplated a grand adventure, a quest for pure revenge, and the dhampirica welcomed it.

# ABOUT THE AUTHOR

For W.J. Cherf, this is his second leap into the marvelous realm of paranormal archaeology, mixed with more than just a dash of contemporary science fiction. His first book of the Adventures of Paranormal Archaeology series, *The Magician's Tomb*, brought screams of delight from his passionate readership.

Cherf is no novice to either archaeology or the ancient world, having excavated in Israel and Greece, along with extensive travel throughout the length of Egypt. Ask him sometime about what a sunrise looks like from atop the Great Pyramid. Or for that matter, walking ancient roads and surveying precarious mountain fortifications in Central Greece. Even better, inquire about a certain Fourth of July celebration atop Tel Beer Sheva in Israel.

As to why Cherf writes in his retirement years, he says, "I always wanted to write a book without footnotes." While this is surely true and is an oblique reference to his treadmill "publish or perish" days in academe, more than that drives the man. On more than one occasion, Cherf has said he has all of these stories in his head, which bedevil him until freed upon the world. In the end, you decide.

For free chapters of Cherf's works, not to mention a handy source for the latest and greatest in Egyptology, go to www.wjcherf.com. Cherf always says, "Sample before you buy." For reviews, go to www.amazon.com and search under "w.j. cherf." If you like this book, review it there. That's how authors find out if they still have the right stuff, straight from their readers.